Egyptian Short

ⓖⓖⓖⓖⓖⓖⓖⓖⓖⓖⓖⓖⓖⓖⓖⓖⓖⓖⓖⓖⓖⓖⓖⓖⓖ

Selected and Translated from the Arabic
by Denys Johnson-Davies

HEINEMANN
LONDON

THREE CONTINENTS PRESS
WASHINGTON D.C.

Heinemann Educational Books Ltd
48 Charles Street, London W1X 8AH

IBADAN NAIROBI LUSAKA
EDINBURGH MELBOURNE TORONTO AUCKLAND
SINGAPORE HONG KONG KUALA LUMPUR
NEW DELHI KINGSTON

ISBN 0 435 90196 6 (AWS)
ISBN 0 435 99408 5 (AA)

© In selection and translation Denys Johnson-Davies 1978
First published 1978

Published in the United States of America 1978
by Three Continents Press
4201 Cathedral Avenue, N.W.
Washington, D.C.

ISBN 0-89410-039-4

Set in Monotype Garamond
Printed in Great Britain by
Cox & Wyman Ltd
London, Fakenham and Reading

Contents

Notes on Authors

Yusuf Idris was born in 1927 in an Egyptian village. He studied medicine and was in practice for a time, later becoming a government health inspector. Though he has written novels and is a playwright of great originality, it is as a short story writer that he is best known in the Arab world. He is essentially a political writer and brings to his stories a unique ability to exploit both the classical and colloquial languages to his literary purposes. Much of his work has been translated into Russian and other East European languages. A volume of his stories will be appearing in the Arab Authors Series.

Yahya Taher Abdullah was born in 1942 in Old Karnak near Luxor. He has had little formal education but is regarded as one of the most promising of the younger generation of writers. He has published three volumes of short stories and one novella; his writing deals mostly with the area in which he was born or with the experiences of people from Upper Egypt who have come to Cairo in search of work.

Edward El-Kharrat was born in 1926 and took a degree in law. Though he has produced only two books of creative writing— volumes of short stories with an interval of fifteen years between them—he is a major influence on the modern literary movement in Egypt. He has translated many works of fiction from English and French, and has also published literary criticism. He has travelled widely in the West, also in Eastern Europe, Africa and Asia.

Ibrahim Aslan, born in 1939, is largely self-educated. He works as a government employee in wireless communications and was recently given a year's leave of absence in which to write a novel.

Abdul Hakim Kassem was born in 1935. He went to secondary school in Tanta and then to Alexandria University. At the end of 1967 he was sentenced to five years' imprisonment by a military court and it was during this time that he wrote 'The Whistle'. After coming out of prison he published his novel *The Seven Days of Man*. He is at present living in East Berlin and writing a thesis on modern Egyptian literature.

Baha Taher was born in 1935 and took a degree in history. He has worked in broadcasting and is at present deputy director of the Second Programme (equivalent to the B.B.C.'s Third Programme).

Lutfi Al-Khouli was born in 1928. He studied law and practised for fifteen years. Since his student days, he has been in and out of prison twelve times because of his left-wing political activities, and has recently made his home in Paris. In 1965 he brought out the leading socialist magazine *At-Tali'a* (*Avant-garde*). He has published two volumes of short stories, three plays and three film scenarios. He has also published several books on political subjects, including *Conversations with Bertrand Russell and Jean-Paul Sartre*.

Mohamed El-Bisatie was born in 1938 and works as a government official. He has published two volumes of short stories and a novel.

Nabil Gorgy was born in Cairo in 1944. He studied civil engineering at Cairo University. He has also studied Egyptology and is interested in mythology and mysticism. He has written three (unpublished) novels in colloquial Arabic and a number of short stories. He has lived and worked in and around New York since 1969.

Naguib Mahfouz, the foremost novelist in the Arab world, was born the son of a merchant in one of the old quarters of Cairo in 1911. He studied philosophy at Cairo University. He started his writing career with several historical novels, and in 1945 wrote the first of his works depicting contemporary Egyptian life. His novels deal mainly with the middle class and the action is generally centred on Cairo. He has published over twenty novels and several volumes of short stories. His early novel *Midaq Alley* is available in the Arab Authors Series, and the publication of several others in translation is planned.

Suleiman Fayyad was born in 1929 in a village in the province of Mansoura. He studied at Al-Azhar University, and his student days there provide the background for his present story. He works as a teacher of Arabic and previously taught in Saudi Arabia. He has published six volumes of stories and one short novel.

Abdul Rahman Fahmy was born in 1924 and studied Arabic literature at Cairo University. Since then he has worked as a teacher of Arabic. He has written seven volumes of short stories and plays, and also writes for broadcasting.

Yusuf Sibai was born in 1917 and graduated from the Military College. For a time he taught military history. Under Nasser and Sadat, he has occupied several important posts, including that of Minister of Culture and Information 1973–6. He is a prolific and popular writer, many of his novels and stories being adapted for the cinema, television and broadcasting.

Sonallah Ibrahim was born in Cairo in 1937. After studying law he worked as a journalist. He spent the years 1959 to 1964 in prison because of his political activities. In 1968 he went to Lebanon, thence to East Berlin and later to Moscow where he studied film making. He recently returned to Cairo. The present story appeared in a volume entitled *The Smell of It*, which will be reissued in the Arab Authors Series.

Yusuf Sharouni was born in 1924 in the Egyptian countryside. He studied philosophy at Cairo University and worked for several years in the Sudan as a teacher. He has published books of short stories, also volumes of criticism on modern Egyptian writing. He works at the Supreme Council for the Arts, Literature and Social Sciences in Cairo.

Yahya Hakki was born in 1905 and took a degree in law. For several years he served in the diplomatic service and travelled widely in Europe. He speaks English, French, Italian and Turkish. An early pioneer of the novella and the short story, he is distinguished for the sensitivity and dexterity with which he employs the Arabic language. His early novella, *The Lamp of Umm Hashem*, is available in translation. Besides many volumes of creative work, he has published a short study of the Egyptian short story.

Gamil Atia Ibrahim was born in Cairo in 1937. He took a diploma in art appreciation at the Academy of Arts and is now preparing an M.A. thesis on art in prehistoric Africa. He taught for two years in Morocco. He has published one volume of short stories.

Denys Johnson-Davies was born in 1922 in Canada. He began studying Arabic at the School of Oriental Studies, London University, in 1937, and later took a degree at Cambridge. He worked for some years in the Arabic section of the B.B.C., lectured at Cairo University and, more recently, was director of an Arabic broadcasting station in the Arabian Gulf. Besides his translations from modern Arabic literature, he is interested in Islamic studies and is co-translator of a volume of the Prophet's Sayings (Hadith). He lives in Cairo.

House of Flesh

Yusuf Idris

The ring is beside the lamp. Silence reigns and ears are blinded. In the silence the finger slides along and slips on the ring. In silence, too, the lamp is put out. Darkness is all around. In the darkness eyes too are blinded.

The widow and her three daughters. The house is a room. The beginning is silence.

* * *

The widow is tall, fair-skinned, slender, thirty-five years of age. Her daughters too are tall and full of life. They never take off their flowing clothes which, whether they be in or out of mourning, are black. The youngest is sixteen, the eldest twenty. They are ugly, having inherited their father's dark-skinned body, full of bulges and curves wrongly disposed; from their mother they have taken hardly anything but her height.

Despite its small size, the room is large enough for them during the daytime; despite the poverty of it, it is neat and tidy, homely with the touches given to it by four females. At night their bodies are scattered about like large heaps of warm, living flesh, some on the bed, some around it, their breathing rising up warm and restless, sometimes deeply drawn.

Silence has reigned ever since the man died. Two years ago the man died after a long illness. Mourning ended but the habits of the mourners stayed on, and of these silence was the most marked, a silence long and interminable, for it was in truth the silence of waiting. The girls grew up and for long they waited expectantly, but the bridegrooms did not come. What madman will knock at the door of the poor and the ugly, particularly if they happen to be orphans? But hope, of course, is present, for—as the proverb says—even a rotten bean finds some blind person to weigh it out, and every girl can find her better half. Be there poverty, there is always someone who is poorer; be there ugliness, there is always someone uglier. Hopes come true, sometimes come true, with patience.

A silence broken only by the sound of reciting from the Koran; the sound rises up, with dull, unimpassioned monotony. It is being given by a Koranic reciter and the reciter is blind. It is for the soul of the deceased and the appointed time for it never changes: Friday afternoons he comes, raps at the door with his stick, gives himself over to the hand stretched out to him, and squats down on the mat. When he finishes he feels around for his sandals, gives a greeting which no one troubles to answer, and takes himself off. By habit he recites, by habit he takes himself off, and so no one is aware of him.

The silence is permanent. Even the breaking of it by the Friday afternoon recital has become like silence broken by silence. It is permanent like the waiting, like hope, a hope that is meagre yet permanent, which is at least hope. However little a thing may be, there is always something less, and they are not on the look-out for anything more; never do they do so.

Silence goes on till something happens. Friday afternoon comes and the reciter does not come, for to every agreement however long it may last there is an end—and the agreement has come to an end.

Only now the widow and her daughters realize what has occurred: it was not merely that his was the only voice that broke the silence but that he was the only man, be it only once a week, who knocked at the door. Other things too they realized: while it was true that he was poor like them, his clothes were always clean, his sandals always polished, his turban always wound with a precision of which people with sound eyesight were incapable, while his voice was strong, deep and resonant.

The suggestion is broached: Why not renew the agreement, right away? Why not send for him this very moment? If he's busy, so what—waiting's nothing new? Towards sunset he comes and recites, and it is as if he recites for the first time. The suggestion evolves: Why doesn't one of us marry a man who fills the house for us with his voice? He is a bachelor, has never married, has sprouted a sparse moustache and is still young. One word leads to another—after all he too is no doubt looking for some nice girl to marry.

The girls make suggestions and the mother looks into their faces so as to determine to whose lot he shall fall, but the faces turn away, suggesting, merely suggesting, saying things without being explicit. Shall we fast and break that fast with a blind man? They are still dreaming of bridegrooms—and normally bridegrooms are men endowed with sight. Poor things, they do not yet know the world of men; it is impossible for them to understand that eyes do not make a man.

'You marry him, Mother. You marry him.'

'I? Shame on you! And what will people say?'

'Let them say what they like. Whatever they say is better than a house in which there is not the sound of men's voices.'

'Marry before you do? Impossible.'

'Is it not better that you marry before us so that men's feet may know the way to our house and that we may marry after you. Marry him. Marry him, Mother.'

She married him. Their number increased by one and their income increased slightly—and a bigger problem came into being.

It is true that the first night passed with the two of them in their bed, but they did not dare, even accidentally, to draw close to one another. The three girls were asleep but from each one of them was focused a pair of searchlights, aimed unerringly across the space between them: searchlights made up of eyes, of ears, of senses. The girls are grown up; they know; they are aware of things, and by their wakeful presence it is as if the room has been changed into broad daylight. During the day, however, there is no reason for them to stay there, and one after the other they sneak out and do not return till around sunset. They return shy and hesitant, moving a step forward, a step back, until, coming closer, they are amazed, thrown into confusion, are made to hasten their steps by the laughter and guffaws of a man interspersed by the giggling of a woman. It must be their mother who is laughing, also laughing is the man whom previously they had always heard behaving so correctly, so properly. Still laughing, she met them with open arms, her head bared, her hair wet and combed out, and still laughing. Her face, which they had instinctively perceived as nothing but a dead lantern where spiders, like wrinkles, had made their nest, had suddenly filled with light; there it was in front of them as bright as an electric bulb. Her eyes were sparkling; they had come forth and shown themselves, bright with tears of laughter; eyes that had previously sought shelter deep down in their sockets.

The silence vanished, completely disappeared. During dinner, before dinner, and after dinner, there are plenty of jokes and stories, also singing, for he has a beautiful voice when he sings and imitates Umm Kulthoum and Abdul Wahhab; his voice is loud and booming, raucous with happiness.

You have done well, Mother. Tomorrow the laughter will attract men, for men are bait for men.

Yes, daughters. Tomorrow men will come, bridegrooms will make their appearance. Yet the fact is that what most occupied her was not men or bridegrooms but that young man—albeit he was blind, for how often are we blind to people just because they are blind—that strong young man full of robust health and life who had made up for her the years of sickness and failure and premature old age.

The silence vanished as though never to return and the clamour of life pervaded the place. The husband was hers, her legitimate right in accordance with the law of God and His Prophet. What, then, was there to be ashamed about when everything he does is lawful? No longer does she even worry about hiding her secrets or being discreet, and even as night comes and they are all together and bodies and souls are set loose, even as the girls are scattered far apart about the room, knowing and understanding, as though nailed to where they are sleeping, all sounds and breathing aquiver, controlling movements and coughs, suddenly deep sighs issue forth and are themselves stifled by more sighs.

She spent her day doing the washing at the houses of the rich, he his day reciting the Koran at the houses of the poor. At first he did not make it a practice to return to the house at midday, but when the nights grew longer and his hours of sleep less, he began to return at midday to rest his body for a while from the toil of the night that had passed and to prepare himself for the night to come. Once, after they had had their fill of the night, he suddenly asked her what had been the matter with her at midday: why was she talking unrestrainedly now and had maintained such complete silence then, why was she now wearing the ring that was so dear to him, it being the only thing by way of bridal money and gifts the marriage had cost him, while she had not been wearing it then?

She could have risen up in horror and screamed, could have gone mad. He could be killed for this, for what he is saying has only one meaning—and what a strange and repulsive meaning.

A choking lump in the throat stifled all this, stifled her very breathing. She kept silent. With ears that had turned into nostrils, tactile sense and eyes, she began listening, her sole concern being to discover the culprit. For some reason she is sure it is the middle one: in her eyes there is a boldness that even bullets cannot kill. She listens. The breathing of the three girls rises up, deep and warm as if fevered; it groans with yearning, hesitates, is broken, as sinful dreams interrupt it. The disturbed breathing changes to a hissing sound, a hissing like the scorching heat that is spat out by thirsty earth. The lump in the throat sinks down deeper, becomes stuck. What she hears is the breathing of the famished. However much she sharpens her senses she is unable to distinguish between one warm, muffled heap of living flesh and another. All are famished; all scream and groan, and the moaning breathes not with breathing but perhaps with shouts for help, perhaps with entreaties, perhaps with something that is even more.

She immersed herself in her second legitimate pursuit and forgot her first, her daughters. Patience became bitter-tasting, even the mirage of bridegrooms no longer made its appearance. Like someone awakened in terror to some mysterious call, she is suddenly stung into attention: the girls are famished. It is true that food is sinful, but hunger is even more so. There is nothing more sinful than hunger. She knows it. Hunger had known her, had dried up her soul, had sucked at her bones; she knows it, and however sated she is, it is impossible for her to forget its taste.

They are famished, and it was she who used to take the piece of food out of her own mouth in order to feed them; she, the mother, whose sole concern it was to feed them even if she herself went hungry. Has she forgotten?

Despite his pressing her to speak, the feeling of choking turned into silence. The mother kept silent and from that moment silence was ever with her.

At breakfast, exactly as she had expected, the middle one was silent—and continued in her silence.

Dinner-time came with the young man happy and blind and

enjoying himself, still joking and singing and laughing, and with no one sharing his laughter but the youngest and the eldest.

Patience is protracted, its bitter taste turns to sickness—and still no one shows up.

One day, the eldest one looks at her mother's ring on her finger, expresses her delight in it. The mother's heart beats fast—and beats yet faster as she asks her if she might wear it for a day, just for one single day. In silence she draws it off her finger; in silence the eldest puts it on her own same finger.

At the next dinner-time the eldest one is silent, refuses to utter. The blind youth is noisy, he sings and he laughs, and only the youngest one joins in with him.

But the youngest one, through patience, through worry, through lack of luck, grows older and begins asking about when her turn will come in the ring game. In silence she achieves her turn.

The ring lies beside the lamp. Silence descends and ears are blinded. In silence the finger whose turn it is stealthily slips on the ring. The lamp is put out: darkness is all-embracing and in the darkness eyes are blinded.

No one remains who is noisy, who tells jokes, who sings, except for the blind young man.

Behind his noisy boisterousness there lurks a desire that almost makes him rebel against the silence and break it to pieces. He too wants to know, wants to know for certain. At first he used to tell himself that it was the nature of women to refuse to stay the same, sometimes radiantly fresh as drops of dew, at other times spent and stale as water in a puddle; sometimes as soft as the touch of rose petals, at other times rough as cactus plants. True, the ring was always there, but it was as if the finger wearing it were a different finger. He all but knows, while they all know for certain, so why does the silence not speak, why does it not utter?

One dinner-time the question sneaks in upon him unawares: What if the silence should utter? What if it should talk?

The mere posing of the question halted the morsel of food in his throat.

From that moment onwards he sought refuge in silence and refused to relinquish it.

In fact it was he who became frightened that sometime by ill chance the silence might be scratched; maybe a word might slip out and the whole edifice of silence come tumbling down—and woe to him should the edifice of silence tumble down!

The strange, different silence in which they all sought refuge.

Intentional silence this time, of which neither poverty nor ugliness nor patient waiting nor despair is the cause.

It is, though, the deepest form of silence, for it is silence agreed upon by the strongest form of agreement—that which is concluded without any agreement.

*   *   *

The widow and her three daughters.

And the house is a room.

And the new silence.

And the Koran reciter who brought that silence with him, and who with silence set about assuring for himself that she who shared his bed was always his wife, all proper and legitimate, the wearer of his ring. Sometimes she grows younger or older, she is soft-skinned or rough, slender or fat—it is solely her concern, the concern of those with sight, it is their responsibility alone in that they possess the boon of knowing things for certain; it is they who are capable of distinguishing while the most he can do is to doubt, a doubt which cannot become certainty without the boon of sight and so long as he is deprived of it just so long will he remain deprived of certainty, for he is blind and no moral responsibility attaches to a blind man?

Or does it?

Grandad Hasan

Yahya Taher Abdullah

It was Grandad Hasan's practice, when the holy month of Ramadan had come in and right through until its thirty glorious days had elapsed, to perform the afternoon prayer in community at the mosque of his grandfather, the late Abdullah, after which he would return and seat himself, to the left of the main door, on the bench that had been built of stones taken from ancient sites.

It was nearly eighty years since this stone bench had been built and Grandad Hasan had first sat on it; since men had gone off with camels to bring back stones fallen from the wall of the ancient temple. And so the house had been constructed in less than a week: a family house in miniature but without an outer wall, a hallway, a guest-room or a mosque, though it did have a stable for horses, also a mill and a press exclusively for Grandad Hasan's family, just as over there they were exclusively for Grandad Abdullah's family. Thus the stone that built both of them had been dragged along by two hefty oxen.

Grandad Hasan had consummated his marriage to Nashwa, the daughter of Hagg Sayyid, and he had had three sons and four daughters by her; when she had died Grandad Hasan had married Hafsa, the daughter of Yusuf Abdul Karim, but she had borne him nothing but daughters, so he had married Zannouba, her younger sister, who became the mother of his boys, Abdul Mageed, Abdul Basit and Abdul Magid, and of two daughters, Amina and Fatima.

On the right of Grandad Hasan the door of the house was closed. He called out: 'Hey, girl!' The door made of sycamore wood gave a low, heavy creaking sound and the large stone rolling along the ground made a muffled noise. It was one of the six young daughters

8

of Grandad Hasan's children who had done this, and now the door stood half-open, held back by the large stone. Which girl was it today? Grandad Hasan asked himself, and he called out: 'Hey, girl!' Nawal, the daughter of the middle son, Abdul Hamid, came along, breathless, her small head held to one side, her thin neck twisted under a small basket filled with dates. She moved the basket from her head to her shoulder, resting it against her knee, then lowered the basket on to the bench and dragged it along till it was beside her grandfather, within reach of his right hand. Nawal went off at a run and came back with another basket containing bread, which she placed beside the basket of fruit. She remained standing without saying anything. Her grandfather did not speak to her; he merely smiled, knowing that she was happy at having done what she had. He remembered that he had not asked her about the opening of the door this time, so he did so. Nawal ran into the house then came back and said: 'It's Insaf, Grandad.' Her grandfather asked her with a stern frown: 'And where are the rest of the girls?' 'Inside, Grandad,' replied Nawal. 'And the boys?' asked her grandfather. 'They're all at home, Grandad,' said Nawal. 'They're all inside, Grandad.'

Grandad Hasan sees the houses stretching out on both sides of the lane. Over there, after Ahmed Rawi's house, the lane takes a turn. That large black form at the turn remains motionless: it looks like a large, black, kneeling camel.

The old men pass by, dismounting if they happen to be riding, and go up to greet him. He returns the greeting in Allah's name and adds joyfully: 'Ramadan is noble', and hears their reply: 'Noble, O son of the noble.' The faces of the men are different, their expressions change, but their reply is one and unchanging: 'Noble, O son of the noble.' Grandad Hasan's sense of well-being increases and he jokes with the young men who come along; as they kiss his hand his body starts up in protest and he asks forgiveness of Allah for every great sin, then goes back to joking with them, calling each by his mother's name. 'Fasting or not, O son of Husniyya?' he said to Salih Sanousi. 'Fasting, thanks be to Allah, Grandad,' replied Salih, and Grandad Hasan knew he was telling the truth. As for Shahhat Fikri, Grandad had withdrawn his hand from between the other's hands, which were just below his mouth as he muttered 'I ask for-giveness of Allah,' then shouted: 'You're not fasting, you're bringing ruin to your religion,' to which Shahhat answered: 'By the honour of Mohammed, I'm fasting—just as you are, Grandad.' The grandfather shouted back in rebuke: 'You son of a dog, don't swear by the Prophet's honour—you don't know his worth. Better swear by the honour of Wadeeda daughter of Sakit, your mother. Off with you! It's written all over your face you're a heathen.' 'By Allah, I'm fasting this year, Grandad,' said Shahhat, smiling, knowing that Grandad Hasan would not stop joking with him and guessing what the grandfather would say to him next. 'You'll say, don't swear by Allah, but, by Allah the Almighty, I'm fasting.' 'Then why,' the grandfather asked him gleefully, 'is your face black?' 'From anger and the sun, Grandad,' said Shahhat, 'but, by Allah the Almighty, I *am* fasting.' Half convinced and half resigned, Grandad Hasan said: 'All right, off you go. You've sworn by Allah. The Lord can blind you or afflict you with some calamity if you've lied. He who has created the vast universe containing both djinn and man, and with all the mountains and trees that are to be seen, is capable of harming you if you've lied. The name of Allah must not be taken in vain, Shahhat.' 'Yes, by Allah, Grandad,' said Shahhat and departed. When Mansour the son of Sadiq passed by, he was asked by the grandfather if he was fasting; he answered in the affirmative, and when he asked him if he used to pray he said: 'No,' and Grandad Hasan exhorted him to pray and scolded him, hurling angry words at him as he went off: 'You son of a donkey, it should be known to you that His reckoning is hard and cannot be endured by a mule like you, nor yet will ten oxen like you endure it.'

And when the women pass by they have to adjust their robes around their mortal bodies and show confusion, and Grandad Hasan will be aware of their confusion of gait and the way their feet drag in the dust that flies up around them. As for that stray dog with no known owner, it passes by Grandad Hasan at this time every day and cocks its hind leg, resting it against the wall of the house opposite, pees, then goes on its way after Grandad Hasan has screamed at it: 'Go away! Off with you, you accursed, ill-omened creature.'

On the two mats spread out in front of the stone bench above the ground that had been sprinkled with water was a place for God's guests on earth, the needy and the deprived. From the basket Grandad Hasan gives out bread with his right hand, while from the basket of dates he scoops up with trembling hand more than can be held in one's palm. 'All good is from Allah,' he would say, 'and is done in order to gain His approval.' Thus the ancestors, those who had journeyed to the House of the True One, had retained the wealth and position they had inherited, so gaining the blessings of this world and Paradise in the next. I in my turn must sense my forefathers' inherited ability to give for the love of Allah, and it will be for my sons to know that the branch of the tree does not approach being good other than with Allah's permission, that this happens only to the few chosen of His worshippers, to those with full hearts.

Time passed and sunset drew near. The black camel rose with its mighty body and walked slowly towards Grandad Hasan. Gradually the houses withdrew from view, first the distant ones, then those close by, while the camel moved on, large and black, towards the grandfather. The grandfather closed his eyes. (The universe was vast, limitless, of a dark blueness, and the deserts were spacious, without bounds, the sands yellow and fiery, and from out of their belly there exploded forth hill upon hill upon hill, a whole series of hills, blood-red like the colour of dusk. Everything now was at the prime virgin state of creation, and the eye of the believer could make out that black spot separating day from night, which looks so small and grows bigger as it draws nearer to the viewer.)

Grandad Hasan's heart grew dry and his failing body shook as he spoke to himself: 'How puny is this human being in Allah's Kingdom!' and he asked himself who the guest might be? Who was that person who was wandering through the earth? The Messenger of Allah who appears from afar as a black spot, who could it be? Was it the Khidr, upon whom be peace, the teacher of Moses? Or could it be the Maghribi? Could it be that cunning, avid one?

The voices of the boys come through with a faint clamour. They are over there at Mohammed ibn Makiyya's shop, and over there is a mulberry tree which is still alive, while Ahmed Mabrouk who planted it died ten years ago. The boys' rowdiness means that the gun for breaking the fast has been heard on the radio of Hagg Mohammed, the eldest of Grandad Hasan's brothers, in accordance with Cairo time. The time has thus come round for breaking the fast for those living under the protection of Sayyida Zeinab and Sayyidna Hussein, and when One-eyed Yusuf gives the call to prayer from high up on the Abdullah mosque the time will have come for the people of both New and Old Karnak to break the fast. Rashad the son of Grandad Kamil, the brother of Grandad Hasan, comes along, flying like a pigeon: 'The time for sunset prayers has come, Grandad,' and Grandad Hasan stretches out his hand and the little boy grasps hold of it and they enter the house.

The spacious courtyard of the house has been spread with mats; the low wooden tables stand on their four legs, no large gaps between them; the brass trays on top of the tables hold dishes of vegetables and meat, also of *kunafa* and the other special sweets for Ramadan. The bulb hanging inside over the door-opening lets fall a cone of light on those seated and casts shadows on all sides, making the time of sunset seem nearer to that of noon.

Here you are, Grandad Hasan, amidst sons and wives of sons and sons of sons, loved and held in reverence, so give thanks to Allah the number of times that there are beads to your silver-inlaid rosary. All await your hand to be stretched forth, the sleeve rolled up, and for you to take up your glass and say: 'In the name of Allah the Merciful, the Compassionate' and drink the infusion of dates. Then you stretch out your hand to the food and the other hands stretch out in turn, and the many noises of mastication and swallowing of food are heard. Suddenly the shadow falls on the dishes, the shadow hides all the empty delights of the soul. You will not think long, Grandad Hasan, for you know by heart what you will say and you know too who it is who approaches.

(Come along in, Master Khidr. This is your house and this is from Allah's bounty. I am the servant of Allah, I am Grandad Hasan. O my Lord Khidr, come in and sit down.) Misgivings come and the body shudders, O Grandad Hasan. Perhaps your guest was the Maghribi, O Grandad Hasan. Perhaps that sly one has come and you will have to bargain with him.

·   ·   ·   ·   ·

Having finished his breakfast, Grandad Hasan takes himself off to the lavatory which lies under the well of the stairway leading up to the second floor of the house. One of his granddaughters will have preceded him there and filled up the brass ewer and have left it in front of the lavatory door so that he can take it in with him, then he will come out, having rid himself of urine and excrement, to be met by a girl carrying a copper ewer and with a basin placed on the floor in which Grandad Hasan will make his ablutions. When he comes to washing his feet he takes up the ewer and pours the water over them, dismissing the girl with a muttered word, and any one of the girls takes over the spreading of one of the many prayer carpets in the house, all of which have been given to Grandad Hasan by those who have visited the holy lands of the Hejaz. On the east side, facing the open main door of the house, Grandad Hasan prays, having driven away every random thought, be it good or evil. Having finished his prayers, he recites the set part of the Koran, after which he remains seated on the soft velvety carpet, until one of the girls brings him a glass of tea and he gives himself up to some thought from which his imagination takes off.

(Each of them comes in ragged clothes, disguised as someone begging, in his hand a staff and on his shoulder a saddle-bag. Anyone meeting up with one of them cannot tell the difference. The Khidr is a great traveller and only the eye of a true believer can see him. When he comes to you in the guise of a beggar and you reject him, the grace of Allah that He has bestowed upon you perishes, but if you are generous to him Allah will be generous to you—and it is the Khidr who taught Moses about the things that are hidden in the earth, Allah's virgin daughter—and you will live happily for ever. Likewise the wily Maghribi knows what form the Khidr takes and so makes himself look like him. Then, taking you unawares, he makes his way to the house—and he is the only one who knows where lies the treasure, perhaps buried by ancestors possessed of many wiles. The vagabond takes you unawares, kills the guardian of the treasure, who is one of the djinn, and the Maghribi disappears with not a trace of him to be found. So, Grandad Hasan, you should be wary about your guest. Treat him hospitably, certainly, but keep a very close eye on his every move. He will come and you will say 'Welcome' and you will offer him what you have. The guest will get up, holding in his hand a large cane. He will go round the house with it, while you keep as close to him as his shadow, as he raises and lowers the cane and counts: One . . . five . . . seven . . . then strikes the ground with the cane and it splits open by permission of its Lord and out comes the gold, the pearl and turquoise necklaces, and all the hidden things of the secret earth. Catch hold of your guest by the collar and look into his eyes. The eyes of the Khidr gleam just like two jewels, for he is a prophet. As for the Maghribi's eyes, they take on a sly look directly they see wealth. If it's the Khidr, O Grandad Hasan, say to him: 'Your pardon, Master,' and kiss his shoulders and rain down upon them tears of remorse. If it is the Maghribi, then bargain with him. If he says 'A half' say 'A quarter', and if he says 'A quarter' say 'An eighth', and so on, Grandad Hasan, for you are a man who has struggled in the world and no one must gain the upper hand of you lightly.)

Now the time has arrived for the evening prayer. Grandad Hasan must make his ablutions anew: 'Allah curse the stomach, it carries nothing but filth.' In a low, grave voice of command Grandad Hasan says: 'Hey, girl,' and in the same tone: 'The ewer, girl,' although he has seen his granddaughter pouring the water into it.

The evening prayer and the special prayers said during the month of Ramadan have come to a close. Sheikh Kamil, the Imam of the mosque of Grandad Abdullah, is in his eighties but looks like a young man in the way he stands and sits: he was never cumbersome in the performance of his prayers. It is like a short dream that has left you, Grandad Hasan. And now you seek sleep and as on every night you are pursued by the vision of noon: three widows, three sisters, daughters of the djinn, their black robes covering them from head to foot, sitting over there under the tamarind trees amidst the hillocks of the graveyards. The great mill turns, it never stops, and the stray dogs howl, the stray cats mew, blood mixes with flesh, and the tamarind trees let fall their flowers under the light strokes of wind, while the eyes of female demons gleam like hot coals.

The grinding machine throbs *tak-tak* unceasingly. Grandad Hasan rises to his feet. Death comes disguised in the garb of lengthy sleep, stealing upon a person and casting upon him an unbearable weight. No eye sees, nor ear hears, nor tongue tastes. Nothing but utter darkness, a darkness that is limitless.

Within the Walls

Edward El-Kharrat

🔲🔲🔲🔲🔲🔲🔲🔲🔲🔲🔲🔲🔲🔲🔲🔲🔲🔲🔲🔲🔲🔲🔲

'Haniyya . . . Haniyya.'

She woke to the sound of the old feeble voice, heavy with the burden of a mother's compassion, the weakness of age and a long, tiring life. The voice came to her through the partly open door, across the atmosphere of the room and its early morning, torpid darkness, with the street light flickering on the wall, faint and attenuated, lacking sharpness. In the room there was still the breath of night, its warm, fetid, imprisoned smell imbued with the odour of sleep.

She tossed and turned on the old mattress, twisting round her thighs the rough, friendly covering which, through its long proximity with her body, had become as it were an intimate part of herself. She could feel it enveloping her as she brought her arms round herself and bent her legs till they pressed up against her breasts. She enjoyed the way her limbs intertwined, enclosing her body within itself, granting it security, finding peace in its familiar, compliant touch: there was no danger in it, rather a moment of security and love. In sheer enjoyment of herself, wrapped around in the rough, snug blanket, she buried her mouth and chin in her lap, her lips touching her knees and thighs, her face sunk into her body. In an upsurging wave of warmth from her resilient flesh, her body grew tranquil; never had it been granted her to feel such nearness, such compliance, such simple pleasure diffused from anything or anyone else. There was nothing that resembled it. Nothing had ever approached such complete and unadulterated fusion. In all other intoxications there was a severance, a disruption that rent every realization, every fulfilment.

This was true even with her mother, who was now waking her

up; enfeebled by age, her voice was lowered to a despairing, laboured compassion.

There now gripped at her heart the gentleness of a daughter who loves her mother and who shares with her in a dangerous enterprise which all but borders on a crime. She felt pity for her because of the obscure threat that hung over them both together; undefined and unknown yet lying in wait for them outside, all around them, and within them too.

Yet despite this her mother lay at a distance from her, was another person. The lines of old age that had ploughed through the flaccid skin of her face had rendered viscid her feeble, vacant eyes and had dried up that knot of salt-coloured hair that dangled from her head and was hidden in an old faded scarf. All this placed an unclosable distance between them and put the tenderness she felt for her mother on a deeper plane, as though it had been conveyed from the sense of some message coming to her from a person she loved but who was far away, living in some other country.

She stretched out on her bed, then coiled herself in a voluptuous movement; she raised her head from between her thighs and brought it up, eyes tight-closed, wrapped around in her sheet, to the lap of her pillow, moist and hot from its night-long contact with her cheek. She breathed in from between the thickness of the mattress and the pillow, from under the coverings, the odour of her body replete with sleep and warmth, an odour kneaded out of the shiftings of flesh and the secretions of night, heavy, pungent and lubricous with the greasiness of entrails and buried lusts. Yes, she had nothing but this body and what it encompassed, this body which filled the whole world so that there was never anything outside of it: the room, the street, people, the sky, were, she sensed—and her sensation, while obscure, was deep—but spans demarcating her body, spans at whose boundaries it ended. Nothing existed outside these boundaries; the whole world lay within the confines of this thing she had. It was all she had and it belonged to her alone, and she could wrap it round in sheets and breathe in its hot, fetid smell, could wallow in its inmost folds.

There had never been anything beyond it. Her husband who used to come to her of a night was rough and desiccated, almost middle-aged, his sweat impregnated with the smell of raw onions, the dust of storehouses and the pungency of dry sacking, for he traded in onions. Even her husband's violations of her she did not feel as encroachments upon herself. The only feeling she had for him was a slight modicum of pity for this abandoned creature who would seek shelter by her side, under her arm, his head, with eyes tight-closed, almost falling upon her breast, prostrate, his life-force drained from him, a dried-up object of old bones, as though he had already died.

He had in fact died two years ago. She had never been able to feel any sense of loss, for at no moment had he ever belonged to her. When she saw him in his winding-sheet, old, puny, shrunken, his lips covered by a slight palish white froth, she had for him only a faint feeling of pity as she stood detached from him, regarding him as from a great distance.

She had returned home to her mother's house. Having a small income from several *kirats* of land, she had pursued the life of a young widow in Upper Egypt, shut in upon herself between the old walls, coming and going between the room on the roof and the kitchen over the stairway.

But her body would rise in rebellion against her and the whole world pulsate with a demand that would not be calmed. This mysterious rebellion of her innermost desires drove her to do things which a girl, in a position like hers in the family, would scarcely do—and the excuse she gave herself was that she was no longer a virgin.

She used to go out visiting with her face unveiled like the town-bred wives of government employees or the modern generation of schoolgirls. She rebelled against that heavy veil the women in the countryside wrapped themselves round with from head to foot, going out in it through the streets, showing hardly more than the pupils of their eyes shining out from this ambulant, black, flowing tent, as though they were forbidden things that must not be seen, as though they were something taboo, incarnate with terrifying, inhuman forces.

Though still of importance, this matter was not a grave one in the town where one did see the wives of government officials and others dressed in European clothes, somewhat provincial to be sure but none the less urban for all that. What was, however, a matter of real gravity was that she would sometimes go, dressed in this manner, to the village where the family land was located, and this constituted the veriest of scandals. However, she was stubborn and, having set her course, nothing would deflect her. Her family—they were Copts—were not exactly from peasant stock but were engaged in commerce and agriculture and used to send their sons to both schools and colleges, several of whom had graduated and were now living in Cairo as doctors, engineers and chemists. The provinces, though, were different and it was not at all proper that Haniyya should behave in this way: even the wives of doctors and lawyers from the family would not dare defy the provincial law that no woman in Upper Egypt—and particularly in a village— should go out without being completely enveloped in her black covering.

Even the lawyers of the family, even its leading members who were men of education, were quite unable to prevail upon her. Her eyes had a sparkle of challenge, a delight in such defiance, while on the corners of her thin, delicate lips there played something akin to faint mockery as though she knew—she who had scarcely completed her primary education—things that none of these people would dare to know, and in this knowledge of hers she was facing up to truths from which they always fled. With the nervous, startled movements of her small body, taut with an almost unquenchable impetuosity, her brazen laugh and confident, graceful womanly walk, she would silence them all, not with words but simply by her presence and the diffusion of her vitality; in fact, she always caused them fear and unease, as though she were placing her finger on closed wounds that were still sensitive and which by her touch she would rekindle, would almost open up, almost revealing to these people the troubled portals to avenues of thinking which their whole lives had been one continuous struggle to repress. Her flashing, unconcerned, nonchalant way of looking at people—like that of a Pharaonic cat—through black eyes opening out on horizons of the body, seeing everything in it and nothing wrong in it, her whole body which knew itself and was not afraid of itself—it was in these things that the danger threatening these people lay, and so they would cover their eyes against it; it was in these things, too, that the danger that encompassed her lay, the danger searching out the extremities of her life.

Her innermost, personal experience was no longer a secret: the news had reached the family, had been spread abroad, of her relationship with that Moslem peasant who used to till their *kirats* of land in the village. The rumours were persistent and damaging, buzzing round people's heads with the obstinacy of flies.

Was it really true that this peasant would sometimes spend the whole night at the house?

Impossible—and her mother?

Had he really been seen coming out at dawn from the narrow street in the sleeping town?

And what was the true reason for his suspicious goings from village to town and his frequent visits to the house?

For going through the accounts? For discussing the state of the crops?

Why did he not go to the leading members of the family whose task it always was to look after such matters? Why go to discuss them with those two women in their cramped, isolated house? And did he, in actual fact, really go there as persistent rumour would have it?

The mother denied every word of it in her feeble, laboured voice, but the girl scarcely heard them out before she was giving that nervous, provocative laugh of hers, rejecting everything in an off-hand fashion, thrusting aside, so lightly and carelessly, such accusations of theirs.

'Haniyya! Get up, girl, it's getting late.'

She raised her head from the pillow, her luxuriant hair hanging round her. No one knew how she had come by that wealth of thick black shining hair on her delicately-featured brown head, making her look like some girl from ancient Egypt.

She threw the bedclothes from her and a waft of the room's warm air drifted up between her legs, naked under her full, black night-dress. She jumped up from the bed. Light and supple, she stood up, feeling the coarse wool of the rug tickling the soles of her feet. She gave herself a strange, special smile.

'What's the time, Ma?'

Yes, she would have to hurry for the heat of day was almost at its height. She had stayed too late in bed.

When she went up to the roof the sky of Upper Egypt fell upon her with a heavy, pent-up suddenness, like a sheet of dark blue lead. Unbearable. The breeze had come to a halt under this sky, as though reined in, rendered almost non-existent by the effort which took up all its strength, the effort of enduring this sky under which it strained, quivering, without a moment's respite, scarcely able to lift its weight at all, as though it were a muscle exerting every ounce of its strength to deal with an enormous load under which it could not relax for an instant.

She crossed the roof-space to the oven-room, as though cleaving a way through a wave of heat and exertion that resisted her with pent-up obstinacy.

She saw her mother hunched up in front of the oven, throwing fuel into it and getting it ready for lighting, propelled by a small, feverish life that was folded in upon itself. She was touched by that sad tenderness which plucked at her heart with a sympathy she had no patience with, with a sensitivity as keen as the contact of a sharp blade, like a sudden wound of intense gentleness.

And yet, despite this, she stopped at the door of the oven-room, greeting her mother from afar. She could never go up to her and encircle her emaciated shoulders with her arms and kiss her, although the desire to do so now agonised her. Such gestures between a mother and daughter are not common with such people, besides she had had no experience of them. She would never know how to deliver to her mother the message of this tenderness that was now cutting a wound into her very soul. Her mother would know nothing of it, and would depart.

She turned round, forcing her way through the heavy, scalding wave of the sky, ever intense with the throbbing of a hot energy that had been spilt out to the last drop.

Its weight grew less as she walked in the shade of the old, closely clustered houses in the main street of the town, treading on the watered earth. For a while the burden of her love for her mother and the burden of the sky were both removed. She hurried through the narrow winding streets with their overhanging houses, sprightly in her European clothes which clung to her slim, firm body, her mind occupied with her errand.

Yesterday news had come to her from Zikri asking her to go to the orchard the next day in order to settle the season's accounts and discuss matters relating to the land with Buktor, her cousin, and with Shefik.

It was always exciting and made her happy to go to the orchard on the family land. It was as though over there she still retained the magic of her childhood outings. Today she was sure to return home with some fruit as a gift and would perhaps be paid some of the money owing to herself and her mother. They could have come to settle the accounts with them at home, it was true, but the idea of the garden and the outing, the cool shade under the huge old trees and the murmur of the scant muddy waters in the narrow channel which, like a curling thread, twisted its way from the water-wheel— that watery, mellow sound in the hot noon, open and exposed to the breeze from outside—all these things moved her deeply within, produced a sensation of yearning and nostalgia, of a desire for release, while at the same time they assuaged her vague fears. Though she was not afraid of these people, her relatives, she felt, while with them, a certain strangeness, as though the blood of one and the same family did not bind them, as though she did not know who they were. Never did she look at their eyes without seeing in them a world which was both faraway and closed to her, a world with which she had no connection. Their never-ending figures, accounts, and preoccupations with harvests and selling, with rents and mortgages, she never even attempted to understand. All this worrying seemed to her senseless and unnecessary drudgery of not the slightest moment. She found the accounting wearisome and boring, and while they were certainly cheating her this did not worry her, although undoubtedly every piastre was of help.

Suddenly she found herself facing the Nile. She stepped down from the road along the bank on to the jetty of the ferry that would carry her across to their land on the other bank and so to the orchard. Standing on the jetty were several men of the effendi class, one of whom wore a tarboosh and a dark suit and carried some papers—he was perhaps a bailiff or somebody in the administration or at the courts; the others were traders, farmers and peasants. One of the peasants was dragging behind him his water-buffalo to take it across the Nile. They were bound for the village which lay at a little distance from the orchard. There were also two women in their heavy black veils, tightly wrapped around in the heat of high noon, buried inside heavy jet-black clothes so that no stranger's eye might see them.

When the ferry came she stepped on to it, feeling its unsteady deck beneath her feet as it swung gently on the shore water. She felt it as it shook under her body, critically balanced, felt that pleasurable sense of slight danger that plays floatingly with a flimsy yet cohesive gentleness on the waters of the Nile.

As the ferry moved off the breeze rose up, coming down from the broad expanse of river with its water flowing under it in calm stateliness. She was conscious of a sense of scarcely perceptible awe, the load of the heavy sky having been taken completely off her, as though the river had some ancient and godlike magic whereby the sky was lifted up off people's shoulders—so long as they remained between its arms—as deep into their chests, freed and exposed to the horizons, they breathed its air, while within themselves there stretched out a vast expansive freedom.

The broad ferry shook above the full swell of the water and the water-buffalo lowed, suddenly raising its head towards the blaze of noon under the sky, then it went back to chewing the cud, letting drip from its mouth on to the deck a long white thread of spittle.

As they neared the other bank, and the palms and other trees, in their closely-grouped clusters, slowly grew bigger, more distinct and defined, something like fear once again gripped at her heart: she was transferring from a familiar world into an unknown land where she was beset with threats lying in wait for her among the luxuriant trees that watched her like hungry eyes from another world. It was as though this river would fling her on to this land and abandon her there; it would reclaim for itself that freedom, that release, that sense of expansion it had momentarily given her, and would go once more on its way, unfathomed, to its destiny which was not that of man.

She alighted on the bank with her small body, which was all she owned in the world, all she owned anywhere, her slim, pulsating body which once again closed round the world, delineating it, defining it, encompassing it. She was aware of the sky suddenly returning and descending upon her. The charm had been broken. As she walked along the dirt track leading to the orchard, the sky dropped upon her like a massive hand, bearing down on her shoulders, almost forcing her into the ground. Yes, she was late: the intense heat of noon had risen, and the air, in its shimmering intensity, was bottled up between the fields of maize surrounding her like walls of high, serried greenness, topped by dust. She was almost stifled, strangled in this dusty air stretched tight between earth and oppressive sky.

The peasants accompanied her along the road for some of the way, with their yellowy-brown faces in which bruised, hungry eyes containing all the sadness, all the muteness, all the misery that has never sought a meaning for itself, opened out—or all but; eyes that had never suspected the existence of anything else; it was a misery that was doltish because of the long time it had been firmly rooted, so long that it had become the very mainstay of life itself. She was aware of their glances following her, full of the dry, hard pain that has forgone all accusation and all desire to understand or to justify, this pain which has nothing at all to it except its solid, wearisome weight, which is unbearable but which, nevertheless, goes on and is borne; not the slightest hope is obtained from it, for it is a pure and unadulterated pain, heedful of nothing but its never-swerving perseverance.

The road branched off and the peasants made their way to the village, while Haniyya took a narrow pathway to the orchard. She was free now of those glances that were cast upon her as though upon some strange animal, uncomprehended too like everything else, for everything surrounding them was unfathomed, they having no desire that it should be otherwise—not even that weight that was the very measure of their lives.

Yes, she now felt she was nothing. These glances that haunted her, were shaped for her by those thin, yellow, blackened faces; and this sky of fearful heaviness once again made her feel she had nothing, not even this body sapped by the noon heat and the throb of exertion in the hot, slow blood, and this sweat to which the dust clung and which oozed out from under the armpits, while within her, was a fear, indeterminate yet forming a small, hard, stubborn knot inside the fabric of her entrails: a fear of the fields, thick, crowded together and with narrow pathways; of the stories of gangs, of killings, abductions and demands for ransom which were everyday occurrences in these narrow tracks between the fields; the attacks of men who moved in on their prey with a primordial and brutal fury, with the defiance of total rejection, with the blood that gambles with the whole of the sky and the earth in a despair that no longer accepts a never-ending submission.

This despair, and the desires of men, were still there. She could feel them clinging to these shoots of intertwined maize covered with light dust. It was as though they had become detached from men, these desperate, racking desires, and had cleaved to the heat of noon: whims that would never be assuaged, never gratified, lusts of defiance and ungovernable desires for abduction and grabbing, for robbery and violence, issuing from the dark corners of souls closed to all inroads, rapes that have acquired a stubborn, intangible, independent life of their own—exhaling into the whole noon their constricting, threatening, inhuman breaths.

As she glanced furtively, pierced by this fear deep within her, at the fields, her insignificance thrust itself upon her and she no longer felt she was of the least value to herself. She continued walking ahead, clinging to the tips of her old courage, clutching at it as at a piece of wood in a sea in which she was drowning.

She walked along in this silent gloom in which there was no space, no air, threading her way through this hot, heavy fullness which no sooner opened up for her to pass through before it closed in again, before her, behind her, on every side, as though, were she to creep into its very heart, it would once again surround her, would not acknowledge her, and on carving her narrow passage through it, would immediately coalesce around her, would deny and reject her continually, would wipe her out.

Suddenly, unexpectedly, she found herself in front of the orchard wall; it was as though it had, in a single instant, risen up at the end of the road out of the dust in front of her, huge with its old massive stones, scarcely affected by the passage of time. The orchard had been handed down to their family from days long ago, perhaps bought by one of her ancestors from some big landowner in a bygone time. It represented a harvest of pride and standing to the whole family, this rich, spacious and ancient orchard on its slightly raised land with its massive, solid wall.

She closed the flap of the old wooden door, which creaked on its rusted hinges. Her feet left the dust of the narrow, suffocating track for an opening into a wide roadway bounded by grasses and thorny esparto under thick, leafy, firmly-muscled trees.

The orchard was empty, silent, vast. From between the towering, knotted boles of trees at the far end there could be seen the old stones of the wall carrying within them an unexpressed, enigmatic message. Suddenly, from the slender acacia trees, the cry of a crow rent the sky, followed by the flapping of wings.

She gazed round the empty expanse and continued on towards the shed at the end of the garden. She felt alone in the world; alone without fear, without hope, without desire, utterly alone as though mankind had never passed across its surface, as though they were some foreign, unthought-of concept, an element alien to the mind, unrelated to it.

The loneliness, the stillness of the earth that exhaled its own special dusty heat, the tracks fashioned as though not made to be walked upon, the water-wheel turning on its own, drawn by the cow with the blindfold over its eyes, unceasingly, since time without beginning, driven by no one as though it had sprung automatically into being, revolving in its endless closed circle.

As she walked towards the shed she felt something approaching relief, something like submission and contentment at this spacious orchard abandoned since eternity, with its ancient trees and their twisted muscles, its broad dusty pathways, its uneven ground, its mounds of earth, its towering, sinuous palm trees, its faraway blue, neutral sky and this wall against which everything came to an end.

She turned and made her way—as though not part of it—towards the shed in which her relatives were awaiting her.

Buktor, her direct cousin, was ten years older than herself; she knew that and kept it in mind as though it were a source of pride, another link that bound them. How strong and solidly-built he was, with that wonderful brown complexion, a directness and severity showing in the lines of his face; in his eyes a look of confidence and self-possession; toweringly tall, incorruptible. He was the most outstanding of the men in the family and the most distinguished-looking. He was the only one among them who had hardly said a word to her about her situation: hardly a question or a word of advice or censure. The most economic of them in words, he was the one who was most condemnatory of her, with his penetrating gaze by which he held sway over her, reducing her to something puny before him. He was too the only one before whom she was aware of a suspicion of fear diffused through her, also of an immense admiration.

As for Shefik, he had returned some years ago from the university. He had given up his European clothes and had found contentment in his house, his lands and his capacious *galabia*. He had become flaccid round the stomach and chin, almost effeminate, while the lineaments of his white and fleshy face were flabby with two small, sleepy eyes beaming out of it. She used always to sense his eyes stripping her naked, desiring her, ranging over her, roving across the surface of her body, without having the courage to touch her or enter into her. They were of the same age and before he had gone to Cairo in his early childhood they used to play together. But he had married that thin, skinny wife of his and had let Haniyya fall to the lot of her elderly husband. He had ensured for himself calm and comfort in his large house, with nights of drinking that ended only with the morning. When Haniyya was ever mentioned he would turn moody, full of abuse and threats.

There remained Zikri. He was the real head of the family, the eldest and foremost of all its numerous men. He never stopped working: hiring out men, entering into temporary share-cropping contracts, engaging in management and agency work, ever on the go, pounding the ground with his hulking feet, his body short and corpulent. Yet his strong personality won respect and his vitality never waned; his hoarse, raucous voice possessed depths of intelligence and not for an instant did he avert his eyes from where lay his profit and interest. He was the one who spoke to her most gently, his voice taking on that paternal, humouring tone as he gave her advice and invited her at least to heed the rumours people were spreading and the family's standing. Mention of the Lord Christ was interwoven in his speech, the honour of fathers, their position as Copts, all fluttering like flags high above his hoarse words which would fall finally into boredom and something resembling indifference.

The three of them would make their accounts with her, each in relation to himself, concerning the season's crop. Yes, she would quickly finish with the calculations and would come away with a couple of pomegranates and a bunch of dates and would then wander round the garden on her own, smelling the afternoon air.

She was slightly, very slightly, surprised she had not noticed the shed before now, those low, broad tumbledown walls covered with dried palm branches and mats and intertwined cotton stalks. She did not notice that these low, dilapidated walls were in fact a shed.

She entered the shed without casting so much as a glance at the abandoned riches she was leaving behind her: those trees and palms vainly stretching skywards, that incessantly turning water-wheel, constant, tireless and silent since time immemorial.

As she stepped inside she was enveloped in a sparse gloom saturated with the smell of earth and humid shade.

She came face to face with the three monsters in the moist, earthy gloom and instantly froze. Every ability to act, even to take a single step forward, left her. She stood by the door, no longer in control of herself: here too it was as if she were looking at herself from afar.

There surrounded them all an awful solemnity that was lethal, final, without release: Shefik with his bright eyes in his fatty face bedewed with a slight sweat, as though, after a long wait, he were ravishing her. Zikri was far off, like a rear tower to this vast, old, enduring edifice now facing her, into which she must enter. Buktor was the buttress of this structure, standing there unhurried and throwing his cigarette to the ground with a calm gesture, towering aloft like some strong young priest in an ancient church; in his brown face lay the noble resolve of a crusader, the hideousness of the sentence and an inevitability that was absolute and from which the idea of flight did not occur to her, for it crushed, without the least effort, all resistance, taking hold of what was her own from the beginning in final and confident possession.

As though in a dream, from the end of this gloom that little by little cleared in a strange light, she heard him say:

'Come here, Haniyya.'

She was unable to open her mouth or move her feet. It seemed to her that she would now, at any instant, collapse: all courage left her, just as though she had never been that forward, scoffing girl going her own way in the midst of the town despite everyone. But she did not fall, and this intimate waiting occupied her to the exclusion of everything else, waiting to fall now, this instant, to the ground. Yet the moments passed and she did not fall but stood there forever suspended over the brink of falling, trembling under a tension that drained her of every faculty, leaving her utterly impotent.

She saw him moving towards her with wide strides that had no impetuosity about them, but rather an imperativeness. She saw the features of his face suddenly close up to her eyes, enlarged a thousand times, in his gaze a tenacity of endless depth. She was conscious of a confused movement and then two hands were suddenly gripping her own, two hands closing over her mouth, two hands encircling her neck, and then her mouth was suddenly being crushed against a powerful chest, her lips being closed for ever, while two hands took hold of her feet so that all at once she was being raised from the ground amidst the bodies of men, suddenly fettered in a net of strong hands and fingers, encircled by living pincers that bit into her limbs, by arms and chests that pressed and encompassed her like walls.

Then, at that precise moment, the thong that had wound itself round her inside was loosed and there burst forth deep within her an intense longing for life, a searing, radiant, irrational flame burning within her with a desire for survival, a yearning for continued existence, a wish to go on being in possession of this body which was now falling a prisoner to the shackles of pressing, relentless hands. She had now erupted into an agglomerate that fought to free itself from living limbs and muscles, struggling and exerting herself against these men, not knowing from where she derived her strength in her determination to escape, her resolve to find freedom, her irrepressible desire to come out under the sky, to flee from these arms and chests. To flee. To flee.

Her voice, with which she wanted to fill the whole wide world, gave out nothing but a rasping rattle that was choked back deep in her throat. Her hands were almost being broken in those of Zikri who was pressing down on her back with his belly until he had her completely in his power. A ghastly, concentrated pressure from fingers of steel was now gripping her throat as she stared up into the dark, violent, tensed face of Buktor with its bulging veins, a face rendered no longer human by the great exertion it made, an exertion of the whole body and the two hands that squeezed, of all the bodies of all men in all lands at all times, an exertion that came as it were from the whole world, closing in upon her, shutting off from her the means of breathing, inexorably choking her, growing tighter each instant, its force becoming heavier, the pressure more insistent. Suddenly she was conscious of two feet passing in between her naked suspended legs, of two hands bearing down on her shoulders in a tight grip in which lay a strange and fatal intoxication. This body of hers, which with all her strength she wanted to break open into flight, was now yielding despite herself to a possessive pressure from another body which had so often stripped her bare with its gaze, yielding to him as though accepting him, subjecting herself to him.

Yet she was still screaming, though no sound issued from her: a silent scream that tore down the whole world and escaped in a defiance that would never accept, would never submit. And with her fettered fists she struck out at the stone of the wall that would not yield to her and at which nevertheless she continued to strike out, pounding and smashing at it so as to break through to the open air outside, to be set free. Her feet kept on beating the ground with a stubborn insistence that would never, never abate.

The men let fall to the ground what remained of her and went out to breathe in the fresh air and smoke a cigarette under the closed and unheeding sky.

The Performer

Ibrahim Aslan

It was night and I was lying on my small bed re-reading the latest letter I'd received from my mother. The light came to me from outside through the large window with the iron bars, tracing clear shapes on my pyjama trousers. It dispersed a little of the darkness from the far corners, and when the drops of water began to drip slowly from the tap into the half-filled basin, I heard the tread of light footsteps.

'We've arranged everything,' said the short man.

I looked at him again, also at the impresario. I saw them sitting in front of me in the slightly dark area, the things placed under their feet. It was not possible for me wholly to make out their features.

'Have you shoes?' said the impresario.

'One pair,' I said.

'Black?'

'Aye.'

'Thank the Lord.' He turned to his companion, then sat up straight. 'Things that look difficult to begin with become easy after a time.'

I started to think about this, but the short man informed me:

'There's nothing that needs any thinking about.'

I glanced around me for the envelope so as to put away my mother's letter. I said:

'But doing that work . . .'

'What work? You won't be doing anything except keep sitting there all the time.'

The other one spread out his arms. 'And you'll get fifty piastres a night for just sitting.'

'Got a shirt?' said the impresario.

'I've got one.'

'White?'

'Aye.'

'Thank the Lord.'

He bent down and took up the package. It was placed alongside the box in front of his feet. He tore open the newspaper that covered it and gave its contents to the short man. A black suit. The short man got up and placed it on the bed, standing in front of me.

'Please take off your pyjamas,' he said.

He began helping me to take them off. When I was standing in my vest and underpants, the impresario came up to me holding my white shirt in his hand. While he made me put it on, the short man had taken hold of the black trousers and was kneeling in front of me. He took hold of my leg, raised it and began putting it in. I balanced against his head with the hand with which I was holding my mother's letter. The impresario leaned over and did up several of the shirt buttons for me. The short man stood up and tucked the ends of the shirt into the black trousers and began pulling them together with difficulty. I sucked in my stomach so that he would be able to do up the top button. When he put out his hand to do up the remaining buttons I backed away, placed my mother's letter on the bed, and did the buttons up myself. At that moment the impresario bent down and got hold of my black shoes from under the bed. I sat down. When I tried to bend over to pick up my socks from inside the shoes, I found it impossible. Once again the short man knelt in front of me and helped me put on the socks, also the shoes, and tied the laces for me. He stood up and so did I. Taking up the black coat in both hands, he went round behind me. Putting my hands behind me, I inserted them into the sleeves that were short on me. Though the coat itself was tight, they managed to close the middle button for me. Leaning forward I saw that the whole of my socks showed below the black trousers. The impresario put his hand to his pocket and took out a black bow tie which he tied round my neck. He arranged the collar of the white shirt for me, then the two of them went off to the far corner. They stood looking at me.

'Excellent,' said the impresario.

'Indeed,' said the other. 'Sit down.'

I seated myself on the edge of the bed.

The impresario put his hand into his coat pocket and produced some papers. He and the other man, who was holding a pen without a top, came towards me.

'This is the work contract.'

He unfolded it in front of my face and the short man gave me the pen and pointed to the bottom of the piece of paper. I signed my name and looked at him. The impresario said:

'This contract requires the owner of the amusement centre always to employ you,' and he folded the paper and returned it to his pocket. 'It requires you on your side to be at his disposal.'

'Congratulations,' said the short man.

He moved to one of the corners, spat, then returned:

'This contract stipulates that you will be paid a pound a night, but you will of course . . .' and he smilingly pointed at the impresario, '. . . give him half and keep the other half for yourself.'

'Have you got a card?'

'I have,' I said.

'An identity card?'

'Aye.'

'Thank the Lord.'

He went to the oblong box which was there and took out the musical instrument and the bow. The short one took hold of me, brought the chair into the middle of the room, and sat me down. The impresario made me hold the musical instrument in my left hand while placing its small chin-rest against my shoulder. The short one took hold of my head, turned it to one side and placed my chin on the edge of the rest.

'Don't move,' he said.

I remained sitting like this. The impresario took hold of my right arm and placed the end of the stringed bow in my hand. He bent my arm until the middle of the bow was above the middle of the instrument. When the strings were touched I heard a faint sound. The two men placed themselves in front of me.

'Don't move from that position,' said the short one.

For the third time he knelt in front of me, brought my knees together and pushed my feet under the chair, then went back to stand alongside the other man. I wasn't able to see them very well because my face was turned the other way, but I could see my pyjama trousers and my mother's letter on the bed.

'Take note of how you're sitting,' said the impresario. 'Note the position of your hands, feet and chin.'

'Have you taken note?' said the other.

'Aye,' I said.

'Good,' he said. 'Now get up and come towards us.'

I got up, carrying the instrument in my left hand and the bow in my right. I went towards them. The short one took hold of me and moved to the door.

'Go and stand outside. When we call you, come in and sit down as you were doing before.'

I went out and stood in front of the door in the dark corridor. After a short while I heard a voice:

'Come in!'

I went in and moved to the chair where I had previously been sitting. Again I saw my pyjama trousers and my mother's letter on the bed.

'Rest your chin,' said the impresario.

I moved my chin.

'Close your knees.'

I closed them.

'Put your feet under the chair.'

I did so.

The short man approached me and raised the elbow of my left arm which was holding the neck of the instrument. The strings were touched and once again I heard the faint sound.

'Excellent,' said the impresario.

'Indeed. Go out once again and don't come in till we call you.'

I went out into the dark corridor. After a short while I heard a voice:

'Come in!'

I went in and moved to the chair where I sat down as I had sat the previous couple of times. I closed my knees and put my feet under the chair.

'Excellent.'

'Indeed. Now imagine yourself entering and walking through a group of musicians. Imagine that there's a long row of chairs in the room. When you enter, slow down a little then move to the third chair from the right and sit down.'

I went into the dark corridor. After a short while I heard the voice:

'Come in!'

I entered, slowed down, then moved to the third chair from the right and seated myself as I had done the previous times. I no longer saw my pyjama trousers and my mother's letter on the bed.

'Excellent.'

'Indeed. Now imagine that you have in front of you a man singing or a woman dancing and that the audience are clapping. When you hear them, raise your chin, bring your face round to the front and lower your hand which is holding the bow. Smile and incline your head twice, then resume your former position. Ready?'

'Now,' said the impresario, 'you hear them clapping.'

I raised my chin and brought my face round to the front.

'Lower the hand which is holding the bow.'

I lowered it.

'Smile.'

I smiled.

'Incline your head twice.'

I did so.

'Now resume your former position.'

I did so.

'They are clapping,' said the impresario.

I raised my chin, brought my face round to the front, lowered my hand which held the bow, inclined my head forward twice, then resumed my former position.

'Excellent. Come here.'

I stood up. The impresario took out some papers from his coat pocket. The short man took the instrument and the bow from my hands and placed them on the bed. He came towards me, holding a pen without a top. The impresario unfolded a small piece of paper before me. The other gave me the pen and pointed with his finger to the bottom of the page. I signed my name and looked at him.

'This,' said the impresario, 'is a receipt for the black coat and trousers, also the bow tie.'

He unfolded another piece of paper in front of me. I signed my name at the bottom of it. He folded up the two pieces of paper and returned them to his coat pocket.

'And this is a receipt for the instrument and the bow.' He looked at his wrist-watch. 'We haven't got much time.'

'Sit on the chair as before,' said the other one.

Carrying the instrument and the bow, I went towards the chair.

'Stop!'

I stopped.

'Where's your chair?'

'The third from the right,' I said.

'Excellent.'

'Indeed. Sit down.'

I went towards the chair and sat down as I had sat the previous times.

'And now,' said the short man, 'move the hand holding the bow. Move it up and down. Bring the strings of the bow right close up to the strings of the instrument. Be careful, though, not to make any sound.'

'Why?' I said.

'Because you don't know how to play.'

I began moving my arm up and down.

'No,' said the impresario. 'Bring the strings of the bow close to those of the instrument without their touching so that the people sitting in the hall think you're really playing.'

Placing the bow closer, I moved it up and down. The strings touched and a loud sound rang out.

'I told you to keep it slightly away.'

I did so.

'Not so much as that. Put it nearer.'

I did so.

'Yes, like that.'

I went on moving the bow up and down.

'Excellent,' said the impresario.

'Indeed. But take note that you'll be doing that for several hours a day.' The strings touched and a loud sound rang out.

'It's no good.'

I stopped. The two men looked at each other.

'Take the strings out of the bow,' said the impresario. 'We haven't got time.'

The short man came up to me, took the bow from my hand and pulled out the strings; the strings on the instrument itself he left.

'But what will people say?' I said.

The impresario laughed.

'They'll applaud you when you play.' He raised a finger: 'But note that the inside of the bow must be towards yourself so that no one notices the strings have been removed.'

'What will the others say?'

'What others?'

'Those who are sitting near me.'

'They'll be playing.'

'Playing?'

'Yes.'

He laughed again.

'Half of them are like you.'

Then his expression changed: 'But be careful—the owner of the place doesn't know.'

'He doesn't know?'

'No.'

'Play.'

I bent over slightly.

The impresario asked me to do something.

The short man asked me to do something else.

The two of them asked me to prepare myself to accompany them there.

A sufficient time must certainly have passed. I had been sitting on my chair as I had done the previous times, playing away without making any sound. The darkness was deep in the far corners. The blurred form of the woman dancing came and went, the large sash round her belly floating lightly in space. Cigarette smoke thickened around me, filling me, making my eyes water. I remembered the latest letter I had received from my mother and made out the sound of the water slowly dripping from the tap into the half-filled basin.

The Whistle

Abdul Hakim Kassem

‹‹‹‹‹‹‹‹‹‹‹‹‹‹‹‹‹‹‹‹‹‹‹‹‹‹‹‹‹

A long, long line of children slips between the maize stalks putting under them small handfuls of chemical fertilizer; behind them is an overseer with a long cane and a whistle.

The boy Hasan and the girl Hanim are at the end of the line, each of them holding a pot full of fertilizer in one hand; their hands, brown and thin, move like the pendulum of a clock between the pot and the roots of the maize.

The weather is heavy, overcast; spiders' webs hang between the stalks and stick to forehead and temple; the maize leaves, like pliant knives, scratch at neck and cheek, while the sweat breaks out festeringly on back and under arms.

The boy Hasan is tense: he strikes at the earth, kicks at the stems of weeds that become entangled with the hem of his *galabia* and implant themselves in the sole of his foot.

He is glancing at the girl Hanim all the time. She is slightly withdrawn, looking warily at him. He leans towards her and she moves away sideways, and ever so gradually they put a great distance between themselves and the other children.

The boy Hasan began to breathe more quickly, glancing more often furtively towards her, while her coquettishness deepened in significance and the small handfuls of fertilizer began to fall not exactly on the roots.

The weather became heavier, more overcast. Hasan knocked against a maize stalk; its ear shook, raising a small cloud of pollen whose motes sparkled in the sunlight above the tufts of stalks. Then it sent down a fine rain that stuck to his already wet face and neck, the runnels of sweat bearing the minute beads to his chest and back, while the solution of chemical salt ran from the palm of his hand down his arm and, both hands being soiled, he was unable to scratch his skin that was ablaze with fire.

He moaned. Lowering his head, he rubbed, with the top of his shoulder, at a drop of sweat slowly making its way along the inflamed skin behind his ear. He gazed long at Hanim, breathing heavily, audibly, through his nose, the girl small under his gaze, her face lowered, and the fertilizer falling very far from the roots.

'Hey, Hanim!'

The girl squatted down on her haunches directly she heard the harsh sound of his breathing, planting the palms of her hands in the ground behind her, the pot of fertilizer thrown down at a slant beside her. Her lower jaw hung down and her lips were parted; a lock of dusty hair clung to her moist forehead; her dress was drawn up, revealing her long red underclothes.

Supporting his weight on his knees and hands, the boy Hasan began moving towards the girl Hanim. Her small breasts rose and fell.

Suddenly they heard the overseer's whistle. Quickly they took up the pots and went on placing the small handfuls of fertilizer under the roots.

The weather grew heavier and more overcast. Violently he pulled away a maize leaf that had almost passed through his eyelid and pierced his eye.

He was slightly ahead of Hanim. He looked around him. They were so far from the rest of the children they heard no sound from them.

He turned and found that he had overlooked several plants. He returned to them and gave them fertilizer. Had the overseer seen it he'd have given him a beating.

There were very many plants to be done before they reached the canal and he could cleanse his hands of the chemical salt solution which bit into them like fire, and scoop up water and splash it on to his face and be able to scratch his festering skin.

A grasshopper landed on the back of his neck; its saw-like leg clung to his skin. He placed the pot on the ground and, hunching up his shoulders, moved his neck frenziedly from right to left, his teeth clenched, unable to bring his soiled hand up to his neck lest he set it ablaze. The grasshopper flew off, landing on a stalk, then to another and yet another, heedless of the overseer's whistle.

The only sound to be heard was that of the monotonous repeated movements of their hands between the pot and the maize stalks. Suddenly the boy Hasan froze where he was; the girl Hanim froze too, as though part of him. He leaned forward, inclining his head to one side, listening. There was nothing except for the movement of cicadas; they were completely alone.

Hasan looked round furtively, having forgotten about the pot of fertilizer he was holding up in the air. He stretched out his free hand little by little till he had clasped the girl's hand violently, his eyes exploring between the stalks of maize. Very slowly the girl Hanim flexed her knees, and Hasan too. A long, staccato whispering noise escaped from his lips, and then the two of them were squatting on the ground, their knees joined, their foreheads almost touching. He wanted to stretch out his hand to her, but it was soiled with that chemical salt, and he began to rub it, with quick, violent movements on the ground, to wipe it clean.

Suddenly they heard the overseer's whistle and Hasan rose to his feet. A broken piece of glass must have cut his finger because it was pouring with blood.

The repeated movements of their hands between pot and roots was taken up again. The salt solution trickled down into the wound. Hasan's hand tightened on the pot as he clenched and unclenched his wounded hand.

Hanim was gazing at him apprehensively, her eyes fixed on his back, while her hand moved between the pot and the maize roots.

Blood poured from his finger, his eyes watered, yet he continued to scoop up the fertilizer and place it under the stalks.

After a while there was a gleam of light between the maize stalks, then he found a splodge of sun on the ground and rose to his feet and ran towards the canal to plunge his face into the water.

Suddenly it Rained

Baha Taher

While they were walking along Kasr El-Nil Street, Samira said, laughing: 'If I were in love with anybody I'd tell you. Believe me.'

'You're lying,' said Midhat—and he declined to give a piastre to a lame beggar who was hopping around behind him.

'I'll get angry,' said Samira.

'But you're right—you've never been in love,' said Midhat.

She stood in front of the shop window: Remnants Week. Something Tasteful for Every Taste. A piece of patterned brown cloth. His face and hers showing in the glass.

'I'm sorry,' he said.

'You never believe me,' she said. 'I want to buy something for Mummy for Mothers' Day.'

'Cloth?'

'No, a bag.'

'I love you,' he whispered. 'What can I do?'

'What are you saying?' she said. 'Speak louder, I can't hear a thing.'

'Nothing. Let's walk.'

Traffic lights. A man with a sad face stared at her. She grasped hold of Midhat's arm then let go.

Alongside her someone said: 'Woman's natural place is in the home,' and his friend answered: 'The man's too.'

The two of them laughed. The traffic lights showed green again. The people on the opposite pavement rushed forward, their faces in a scowl.

'What do you think about going off to Alexandria?' Midhat said suddenly. 'I love the sea.'

'When?' she said.

'Now.'

'And your work?'

'So what.'

'And my mother?'

'So what.'

'Crazy!'

A police squad-car. People walking on the pavements twist round their heads, following the siren.

'I love the desert,' she said. 'I'd like to live out by the pyramids. I hate crowds.'

'Good God, how I hate crowds! When I'm being suffocated by people in the bus in the morning, I'd just like to die. What do you think of this bag? Will it do for Mummy?'

'It's a bit young for her.'

'Mummy's not old. When she walks in the street with me people think she's my elder sister.'

'What fun!'

'What are you saying? Why don't you speak louder?'

'Buy it—I'm telling you, buy it, buy it, buy it.'

'No, it's too expensive. Don't shout like that.'

'What's love?' he said to her in Liberation Square.

She rolled her eyes heavenwards and said: 'In songs and films. Do you think it's going to rain?'

The sky was packed with small round pieces of dark cloud, their edges soft and transparent, swiftly racing through the sky then vanishing like smoke.

'No,' he said, 'it won't rain.'

'I think it will.'

'Perhaps, but listen—I love you. What can I do about it?'

'There's no point in saying such things.'

'But why not?'

'There's no point. I'll get angry.'

They walked along in silence. At Kasr El-Nil Bridge the lion was frowning; there were bird droppings, white as lime, on the lioness. On the lion's eyes too. They walked along the bridge in silence.

'Why can't we be like brother and sister?' she said to him after a while.

He laughed and lit a cigarette.

'You're my brother and I'm your sister,' she said.

He laughed again and she said: 'What makes you laugh?'

Then it began to drizzle and she said: 'I told you it would rain.'

'Yes,' he said—and he threw the wet cigarette in the river.

'You didn't want to believe me and here you are it's begun to rain.'

'Yes.'

'I said so.'

'Yes, you said it was going to rain and I said that it wouldn't rain and it's begun to rain, what exactly do you want me to do about it? Hurl myself into the river?'

'Not at all, just listen to what I say from now on.'

'Become your brother?'

'Let's walk quickly, it's coming on hard.'

'I don't love you either.'

'Yes.'

'I used . . . I used to want to love you, but . . .'

'It's not important, there's no point in saying such things now. Hurry up.'

When they reached the door of the riverside café, she was breathless and there were drops of rain on her cheeks and eyebrows and on a lock of her wet hair that stuck to her brown cheek. He stretched out his hand and wiped away the rain, but she quickly drew back and said: 'Thanks, I've got a handkerchief.'

They sat under the awning in the café while small drops of rain fell on to the river and the grey waves were in a constant state of quick agitation.

'Oh God, I hate drizzle,' she said. 'If only it would pour down we'd be over with it quickly, but this drizzle . . .'

He raised his eyes to the bridge and saw the people hurrying along, their bodies inclined forward, newspapers spread over their heads. The rain looked like slanting transparent lines that filled the universe.

'Yes, it will go on for ever,' he said.

'What will?'

'The drizzle.'

'What do you mean?'

'Nothing.'

A wet black cat streaked swiftly by. Under the nearby table it shook itself and sat down quietly and, encircling its shining black body with its large tail, proceeded to gaze at him with green, enquiring eyes.

The Man Who Saw the Sole of His Left Foot in a Cracked Mirror

Lutfi Al-Khouli

At a quarter to five on Sunday afternoon—as shown by his wrist-watch the hands of which lit up when night fell—the weather was unbearably hot, but what was he to do? The weather—captive—was doomed to be as hot as hell-fire, while he—free—was doomed to live in such weather. Each of them, for some reason or other he did not know and had no desire to pursue, hated the other but they were at the same time shackled to each other like the blacks and the whites in New York. There is no escaping one's doom.

*   *   *

The most absurd thing about this heat was that it imitated the cold: it pierced the skin with feverish pricks when, instead of the burning stings that caused the body to retreat hedgehog-wise into itself, springs of viscid water oozed out of it. A week ago he had discovered by chance that Nadia—who was more or less his wife—had been unfaithful to him with Hamid, his handsome friend with the blond moustache and the laugh that hung with surprising persistence between the elongated nose, as though borrowed from Cyrano de Bergerac, and the slightly drooping lower lip, thus providing his evenly spaced teeth with the chance of showing off their sparkle. It had occurred to him more than once to ask him the name of the toothpaste he used, but when he was about to utter the words he finally renounced the idea. Of what importance was it? Had his brother Waleed been in his place, he would have asked Hamid the very moment the question-mark passed through his mind. He was constantly sowing question-marks around himself so that the world might seem to him a garden verdant with questions.

43

No. The matter was not one of doubts alone. Why doubt or not doubt when he possessed enough bits of evidence to keep his certainty warm? And because certainty is comforting, he felt nothing out of the ordinary about the matter. To be exact, he was not concerned with feeling anything, either ordinary or out of the ordinary. During this week, he had twice caught himself in the act of flagrantly asking: 'Is there still the possibility of feeling something—anything?' He awaited the answer. But nothing in him gave utterance. Within him silence had for long been howling, as though it were an unknown wind in a lost desert. Was there some new epidemic that had spread through the world extinguishing the lights and gagging the feelings inside those born of Adam and Eve? Well and good, the head has landed on the axe—or the axe on the head. He knows not how they say it exactly, this phrase as oddly constructed as one of Salvador Dali's pictures, utterly abstract. Everything in the world has a function, a role, yet even so it is something abstract. A world complete in itself in which is to be found beauty, the square, sex, the straight line, fire and death. Cigarettes. Hamid's nose. Air. Water. Nadia's navel. Music. The sky. Waheed's questions. Newspapers. Reality. And in reality Nadia's infidelity has become a reality. An abstract something that breathes with him this unbearably hot weather. What should he do? Pretty Nadia was still—despite Hamid—pretty; when she winked, flirted and smiled, all the stones of the pyramids of Khufu smiled—and particularly in those moments which, despite their being repeated, are always newly created and in which the awareness of pleasure mingles with the unawareness of pain, and which at that moment soak up everything in the rose-coloured room with the large cracked mirror fixed alongside the window, painted in such sombre hue as though suffering a perpetual bashfulness. How many times had he caught sight, from a fleeting glance in the mirror, of the sole of his left foot as it painfully thudded against the bed with the spasms of his body. Had it not been for this cracked mirror he would never have succeeded in knowing that the sole of his left foot was so white. And his friend Hamid is still—despite Nadia—his friend with whom he spends long nights loafing about the endless streets of Cairo, chattering away like a waterfall. Yet he was as light as a feather, one didn't feel him. From time to time he told him some jokes in which brains and thighs were stripped bare, in the manner of an English lord, rolling the words on his tongue in drawling Arabic.

*　　*　　*

Sweat oozed out incessantly from under his skin, flowing down his broad forehead and pervading the furrows of his face; beads of it rained down, drop by drop, on to his thick eyebrows in a monotonous rhythm, like the sighings of Abdul Wahhab in his song 'The Gondola': his eyes would fill up and stop focusing till he was almost unable to see, when he would sluggishly move his hand with the handkerchief, irritably mopping up the sweat. For two years he didn't remember—despite everything he related, guessed and knew —ever using his handkerchief to wipe away even one solitary tear flowing from his eyes. That was true. For two years he had not known tears: the dryness of indifference had befallen him. Most likely this was connected with his twin brother Waleed who had not returned from his ill-fated trip into the desert. It was said that thirst was the cause—and God knows best. No more than six minutes younger than him, he was, nevertheless, stronger. This was neither false modesty nor a stupid desire for futile lamentation. In this Waleed there dwelt the courage of Samson and Socrates, of Saladin, Byron and Guevara in their love for life and their disdain of death. Waleed used to see millions of things that he himself did not see, and sometimes he would make fun of him because he saw things with his eyes alone—and the eye does not see everything in things. A rose is a rose for all people at all times, even ours, and in every place, even in the desert; but a rose in the eyes of Waleed was a-thousand-and-one things: Nefertiti's eyes, the melodies of Bach, the sun's kiss on the sea at its setting on the platinum beach of Agami, the murmuring of 'I love you' between a man and a woman. When he used to dream of a morrow in which people would be as equal as the teeth of a comb, his voice would become white. When the three men came and knocked at his door one night as he was on the point of going off to Nadia in the rose-coloured room, they entered unhurriedly, lowering their eyelids and softly dragging their feet. This was because they either thought of themselves— rightly or wrongly—as angels of mercy, or because they feared to wake somebody up, though the house was as empty and desolate as a new grave not yet inhabited by the corpse of a man. They cleared their throats more than once in no fixed order, and it was perhaps this that had put them in a state of disjointed hemming and hawing, like the instruments of an orchestra tuning up. They exchanged colourless glances. This it appears was the signal for one of them to stand up. He lifted his body from his chair and surprised him with its great height. Where had he been hiding it? He looked at the man, at the agitated Adam's apple in the middle of his neck with the swelling blue vein. Had Waleed been at hand he would have asked him in no uncertain terms: 'What's all this about, my dear fellow?' But Waleed was not present. This man had come with the two other men instead of him. Three in exchange for one. The tallest of them was standing upright in front of him, like an actor on a stage without an audience. Who does he think he is? Most likely Othello, reciting from memory cadenced words that bring to the ear the sound of drumbeats and the blaring of a brass trumpet. Between one moment and the next, the name Waleed was squeezed in without relevance. With a little effort he would have been able to understand something of what the man was saying, but he didn't attempt to. Why? He didn't ask himself. At last, when one after the one they had pressed his hand, they presented him with Waleed's watch, the hands of which lit up at nightfall. Handling it gently, he looked at it hard, and shook it twice to test it before quietly fixing it round his wrist. They were visibly much affected. Why? Likewise he did not ask himself. He shook them by the hand with a neutral glance and walked with them a couple of steps, nay three, towards the door. When the threshold had become a trustworthy frontier between him and them which they would not step across again, he said to them with a smile which, it seemed from the clouds that drifted about their faces, they did not receive kindly: 'I thank you. Now I have a watch with hands which light up at nightfall,' and they went away. For some moments he stayed where he was. The door was open to the darkness of the street. The light in the house was ravishing the furniture whose anarchy drew out from it, on to the floor and walls, dead, droll shadows. A minute or two of the silence of nothingness, then with firm steps he moved outside, shutting the door behind him on the light with its dead, droll creations, and hurried off to Nadia. That night he enjoyed more than once the sight of the sole of his left foot clearly seen on the surface of the cracked mirror in the rose-coloured room. And when Nadia languidly asked him, as she redid her hair which had the colour and taste of Italian espresso coffee, about the watch he was wearing and was it new, he didn't know how to answer her. However, in a toneless, enigmatic voice he said to her: 'Its hands light up at nightfall.' He wasn't sad. Likewise he wasn't happy.

* * *

The sun's rays were loitering here and there with provoking slowness, like a policeman on his beat who must return to the station with some customers. Its blazing imprints lay on the fronts of the houses, the branches of trees, the lamp-posts that had not yet awakened, and on some turnings up and down which cars, bicycles, lorries and pedestrians' feet made their way to and fro. Ugh! This life never stops, is indefatigable—and his eyes fell upon a compact mass of light reflected from a shop window displaying all sorts and kinds of ties. With suppressed irritation he stopped, rubbing his eyes, and without knowing it found himself gazing at the window. Behind the glass stood an elegant man, elegant as a picture in a fashion magazine, examining dozens of ties, gripped by the confusion of having to choose. Choosing is always difficult, sometimes impossible, and in general causes problems. 'Any tie's all right' he once said to Nadia when she noticed he wasn't good at choosing ties. Hamid's ties were always very carefully chosen. That day a week ago, when he had met him on the stairs of Nadia's house, hurrying to the street as he finished doing up a couple of buttons of his grey trousers, his tie was hanging down on to his chest, the tie with its desert-sand colours and scattered oases of green, and he had smelt Nadia's intimate smell on it. She had certainly tied it for him as she had kissed him and said 'Hurry.' 'Speed is the hallmark of the age,' Waleed was always saying. He had asked Hamid nothing; it was Hamid who had asked him with brilliantly contrived surprise: 'You! Where are you off to?' 'To Nadia.' 'Ah! Nadia lives here?' Without having asked him for an explanation, by gesture, word or look, Hamid had voluntarily justified his presence in the house by saying that he was looking for an empty flat and began weaving detail after detail: How he'd known. Where he'd come from. What he'd found. Even the name of the agent he hadn't failed to mention. All the while, he had stood unconcernedly pretending to listen. He had wanted to pat Hamid on the shoulder and whisper to him: 'Everything you say is plausible. I believe you. I would believe you even if you were to tell me you were naked with Nadia on the bed waiting to board the Giza train when it came into the rose-coloured room through the window,' but between wanting and doing lie impassable seas and deserts. Finally, angelic silence had descended upon Hamid. He had heard him swallowing his spittle before asking: 'What's the time? I'm late for an important appointment.' He had stretched out to him his hand with the watch whose hands lit up at nightfall. Hamid, casting a hurried glance at them and jumping with the nimbleness of a rabbit towards the street, had said: 'So long, my friend.' Nodding his head without a word, he had begun climbing the stairs, step by step, to Nadia. Hamid had been in every corner of the rose-coloured room: on the bed, behind the door, by the window. He had not only been conscious of him when he caught sight of the sole of his left foot in the cracked mirror as the bed gave its traditional tremors, but it had seemed to him that he had asked himself: Did Hamid also see the sole of his left foot? He didn't know what had happened after that because he had sunk into a deep sleep from which he had awoken only when Nadia had roused him in the morning with a cup of coffee. It hadn't been quite hot enough, as at all other times, but he had drained it to the bottom and gone down to the street. In the street girls, carts, cats, soldiers, old men, dogs and traffic-lights had all been frenziedly propelled into motion with the speed of someone convinced he is living the last day in the life of mankind. On the pavement there had suddenly sprung up before him the fat newspaper seller—as though an enchanted earth had cracked open to reveal him. When he had waved in his face a newspaper crowned with red banner headlines and shouted, 'They've got to the moon,' he remembered that he should go to his work at the tram company. He went. What could he do? He had to go.

*   *   *

The weather began collecting its forces of cool air and rebelling against the heat. The strong, lofty sun remained the overlord, the ruler, for the whole of the day, its first steps of withdrawal towards its ordained defeat beginning with the counter-attack of the night.

48

Several soft breezes took courage to stir and the small branches of trees shook. Little birds twittered during the moment when the blood of the wounded sun was spilt across the horizon. Blood— what is now the colour of blood? Is blood still that warm dark red colour or has it changed? He had not yet seen Waleed's blood, so how could he know? But this thing squirming about in front of him like a snake on the asphalt road, as though searching out a prey, is it not blood? And this crazy lorry, disappearing with the devilish bend of the road, has thrown to the ground the man with the white galabia and hair and has gone on its way. Inevitably it has gone on its way, the road being clear and unblocked in front of it. From under the white galabia emerges this red snake that runs towards him with strange defiance. Everything happens with meticulous method as though previously arranged. What should he do? The darkness of night falls above his head. Who is it who calls to him 'Help me'? Whence comes that soft husky voice, reminiscent of Nadia's the day he discovered her infidelity with Hamid? 'The man's blood has been soaked up by the dust.' What's this? What's happened? Where is the man with his white galabia and his red snake? The sun too has fled. The sweat has dried. Those who are running and shoving each other aside as though the end of the world has come, as though the war of Good and Evil has broken out, thrust him once to the right, once to the left, the only word on their lips being 'ambulance', while he remains rooted to the ground unable to move. Millions of ants creep in single file under his skin with the army of darkness whose moment of victory has drawn near. Bells ring out jubilantly from afar as though being tolled at the end of the world, their reverberation growing louder and louder until they seem to be ringing deep inside him. Has his head changed into a belfry? Voices shout out: 'Careful—What's wrong?—The man's gone crazy.' Voluntarily or involuntarily, he was running forward two steps, turning round, standing for a moment listening, then running, then coming back, then standing, then running. The voices—and with them an unknown and faceless enemy—were chasing him, almost catching him. They did actually catch him. He felt a sharp blow on his right side. The voices shrieked 'God Almighty!' He opened his eyes to see what had happened, and he gently brushed against the sky, upright, high and faraway with the moon. The stars, though, were so close that scarcely a hand's span separated them from him. What if I were to stretch out my arm and pluck a star to give to Nadia? No, to Waleed. But where to find Waleed in the lost desert? Should he ask the three men? They wouldn't know and even if they did they wouldn't say. No. He would give it to Nadia to hang above the cracked mirror or even on the end of Hamid's nose. Certainly not. He would put it in safe keeping to give to the one who would certainly go one day and bring back Waleed. What is that moving above his head? Where is his head? Had the stars begun to have gates that opened and closed? Mouths with tongues were moulding words, screwing them up into balls and hurling them into his face. He heard, or imagined he heard, a voice with bent back, leaning on a stick: 'What a life! The ambulance came to the rescue of someone and ran over some-one else.' He understood nothing. Who was the ambulance supposed to rescue? And who had the ambulance run over? And since when did ambulances come? A full, hot hand landed on his forehead, as though it were a left-over from the unbearable heat; in a green voice it said: 'How are you feeling?' He wanted to open his mouth to say something he wanted to say, but he only opened his eyes again. He didn't know whether they spoke or not. When he heard another voice like his own asking the time, he moved his hand so as to indicate his watch. Strange, it was not the same movement of his hand as he was accustomed to make whenever he consulted his watch. He saw nothing but total darkness. Where is the watch? He felt for it with the fingers of his other hand. It was there, lying securely round his wrist. At that moment a screaming buzzed in his ears; he felt it issuing from something awakening suddenly deep inside him. Most assuredly it was his own scream: Night has fallen and the hands of the watch do not light up. His shrieks were con-tinuous like the screaming of a newborn child: Why, Waleed? Why? The 'why' stuck to his tongue, violently bumping against the wall of night, imbued with every desire to destroy it. When they raised him up on the stretcher to the ambulance, they noticed a tear welling up in the twin lakes of his eyes. A young woman, with a radiant expression and clad in black, who had squeezed her body into the middle of the crowd, whispered: 'The young man, poor thing, is crying.' No one, though, knew that it was his first tear for two years.

A Conversation from the Third Floor

Mohamed El-Bisatie

She came to the place for the second time. The policeman stared down at her from his horse.

The time was afternoon. The yellow-coloured wall stretched right along the road. Inside the wall was a large rectangular three-storey building; its small identical windows looked more like dark apertures. The woman stood a few paces away from the horse. The policeman looked behind him at the windows, then at the woman. He placed both hands on the pommel of the saddle and closed his eyes. After a while the horse moved. It was standing halfway down the street. Then, a moment later, it made a half-turn and once again stood itself at the top of the street.

The woman came two steps forward. The horse bent one of its forelegs, then gently lowered it.

'Sergeant, please, just let me say two words to him.'

His eyes remained closed, his hands motionless on the pommel.

Above the wall stretched a fencing of barbed wire at the end of which was a wooden tower. Inside there stood an armed soldier.

The woman took another step forward.

'You see, he's been transferred. . . .'

The sun had passed beyond the central point in the sky. Despite this the weather was still hot. A narrow patch of shade lay at the bottom of the wall.

The woman transferred the child to her shoulder.

When she again looked at the policeman's face, she noticed two thin lines of sweat on his forehead.

Quietly she moved away from in front of the horse and walked beside the wall. About halfway along it she sat down on a heap of stones opposite the building.

The prisoners' washing, hung by the arms and legs, could be seen outside the bars of the windows. Mostly it was completely motionless, even with the breeze that blew from time to time.

The woman whispered to herself: 'They must be wet.'

She placed the child in her lap. For a moment her eyes fastened on a *galabia* that gently swayed to the movement of the wind. She stretched out her leg and gazed at her toes and the dried mud that clung to them. She rubbed her feet together, then gazed at them once again.

Putting back her head, she looked up at the windows of the third floor with half-closed eyes.

The soldier in the tower took a step forward. He rested his head against the edge of the wooden wall.

He looked at the sky, at the roofs of the houses, at the street, then at the head of the white horse.

Suddenly a shout broke the silence. The woman quickly drew back her leg. She caught sight of a bare arm waving from between the bars of a window on the third floor.

'Aziza! Aziza! It's Ashour.'

She moved a step nearer to the wall and stared in silence at the window.

'It's Ashour, Aziza. Ashour.'

She saw his other arm stretching out through the window. She searched with her eyes for something between the two arms and succeeded in making out a face pressed between the two bars. Other faces could be seen above and alongside him.

'Aziza, I've been transferred. Did you get my letter? In four days I'll be transferred. Did you prune the two date palms? Where are Hamid and Saniyya? Why didn't you bring them with you? I'm being transferred. Where's Hamid?'

He turned round suddenly, shouting:

'Stop it, you bastards!'

She heard him shouting and saw the faces disappear from the window. After a while his face was again looking out through the bars, then the other faces looked out above his.

'Aziza!'

She looked at the policeman on the horse, then at the soldier in the tower.

'Who are you holding? Shakir? Aziza!' She shook her head twice.

'Lift him up. Lift him up high.'

She took the child between her hands and lifted him above her head.

She noticed his arms suddenly being withdrawn inside and his hands gripping the iron bars of the window. Then his face disappeared from view. For a while she searched for him among the faces that looked down. She lowered her arms a little and heard shouts of laughter from the window. She spotted his arm once again stretching outwards, then his face appeared clearly in the middle.

'Up, Aziza. Up. Face him towards the sun so I can see him.' She lowered her arms for a moment, then raised him up again, turning his face towards the sun. The child closed his eyes and burst out crying.

'He's crying.'

He turned round, laughing.

'The boy's crying! The little so-and-so! Aziza, woman, keep him crying!'

He cupped his hand round his mouth and shouted: 'Let him cry!'

Again he laughed. A few shouts went up around him. She heard their words and shoutings. Then she saw his large nose poking out through the bars.

'Woman! Don't be silly, that's enough! Cover the boy—he'll get sunstroke!'

She hugged the child to her chest and saw the soldier withdrawing inside the tower.

'Did you prune the two date palms?'

She shook her head.

'Why not? Why don't you talk? I'm being transferred. Pass by Abu Ismail and tell him I send him my best wishes—he'll do it as a favour and prune the trees, then you can bring along a few dates. Did you bring the cigarettes?'

She made a sign with her hand.

'Talk. What are you saying?'

'You've got 'em.'

'Louder, woman.'

'You've got 'em, I sent them to you.'

'When?'

'Just now.'

'Just now? Here, hang on—don't move.'

He disappeared suddenly. Two faces remained at the window. One of them stretched out his arm; he made an obscene movement in the air with his hand. She lowered her eyes, then went back to the pile of stones.

'Aziza!'

Though she did not recognize the voice, she looked up at the window. She saw the man was smiling, his arm still moving about. The second man was kneeling, having raised his galabia above his thighs. She heard him call out:

'Aziza, look!'

She smiled. The policeman was still sitting on his horse as though asleep. From the side window of the tower she had a partial view of the soldier's head. He had taken off his helmet.

She heard several voices calling her. She listened attentively, concentrating her gaze on the soldier's head as he moved within the opening of the window. The calls were repeated, interspersed with abuse. The soldier put on his helmet, but remained inside the tower.

Suddenly the voices were silent and some moments later there came to her the breathless voice of her husband:

'Aziza? I said five—didn't I tell you five packets?' She stared up towards him in silence.

'Woman, what's the use of three packets?' She gestured to him with her hand.

'What are you saying?'

'Five—I sent five.'

'Five?' he shouted fiercely. 'The bastards!'

He disappeared suddenly, then leant out again shouting:

'Wait! Don't go!'

She turned her face towards the window of the tower. He was away for a while, then he returned.

'It's all right, Aziza. Never mind. Five—yes, there were five. Never mind, a couple got taken, it doesn't matter. Listen—what was I going to say?' Silence. She saw him staring out in silence from the window. She shook out her black galabia and walked forward towards the wall. He smiled.

'Aziza, I was thinking of saying something to you.'

Again there was silence. She turned away her head so that part of her face was against the sun. She shifted her head-veil slightly from her head.

'They took a couple of packets. Never mind, Aziza. Never mind.'

He laughed. His voice had become calm. The other faces disappeared from above him, only a single face remaining alongside his.

'Did you build the wall?'

'Not yet.'

'Why not?'

'When Uncle Ahmed lights the furnace, I'll get some bricks from him.'

'All right. Be careful on the tram. Look after the boy.'

She remained standing.

'Anything you want?'

'No.'

She gazed at his face, his large nose, his bare arms. She smiled. The face next to his smiled back.

Suddenly he shouted. 'Did you get the letter? I'm being transferred.'

'Where to?'

'I don't know.'

'When?'

'You see, they're pulling down the prison.'

'Where will you go?'

'God knows—anywhere. No one knows.'

'When?'

'In two or three days. Don't come here again. I'll let you know when I'm transferred. Has the boy gone to sleep?'

'No, he's awake.'

He stared back for a while in silence.

'Aziza!'

Again there was silence. The face alongside his smiled, then slowly slid back inside and disappeared. Her husband remained silent, his arms around the bars.

Suddenly he glanced behind him and quickly drew in his arms. He signalled to her to move away, then disappeared from the window.

She stepped back, though she remained standing looking up at the window.

After a while she seated herself on the stones and stretched out her leg. Taking out her breasts, she suckled her child.

The shadow advanced halfway across the street. She saw that its fringe was touching her foot. She drew her foot back a little. The place was quiet and the washing that had been hung out gently swayed in the breeze.

When she looked at her foot again, she saw that the shadow clothed the tips of her toes. She stood up.

The soldier was still inside the tower; the toe of his boot could be seen at the edge of the wooden platform. Before reaching where the horse stood she glanced behind her, but the window was empty.

She looked quietly at the policeman: his eyes were closed, his hands on the pommel of the saddle. The horse stood motionless.

She walked down the narrow passageway towards the main street.

Yusuf Murad Morcos

Nabil Gorgy

೦೦೦೦೦೦೦೦೦೦೦೦೦೦೦೦೦೦೦೦೦೦

All credit for my marriage goes to my cousin Dr Anis Salama, who acquired his education abroad and obtained a doctorate in pure mathematics from Leeds University in England.

After the death of my father, who died a year before I completed my secondary education, my uncle Salama decided I should move to his house in Cairo so that I could complete my university studies, and before the end of the same year my mother married Mr Riyad Iskandar, who was an old friend of my father's and the owner of the only chemist's shop in the town of Beni Mazar. (Mr Riyad's eyebrows joined up above his nose.)

Death snatched my father away without warning. He was attacked by a sudden sharp pain in the stomach and he went on vomiting for three hours; before the end of this time blood burst out from his mouth as he tried to throw up what was in his intestines. It was said he had been poisoned or had eaten some poisoned food. Coughing up his intestines, my father died.

My uncle's house, with the large balcony on the front, used to overlook the Kubbeh Palace gardens, and when I was a child I would take delight in jumping over its wall into the garden.

'Let's hope you'll break your back, you monkey,' was how my uncle used to rebuke me each time he spotted me jumping over the balcony wall. 'Why don't you follow the example of your cousin Anis, you little devil,' said my father to me the day I fell on my arm and cried with the pain, while over there in a corner of the balcony sat Anis reading as quietly as someone not of his age. He neither laughed nor was sad.

Every summer we were in the habit of visiting my uncle and spending three weeks with him in Cairo, after which we would return to Beni Mazar where my father had his clinic: Dr Murad Morcos, ear, nose, and throat specialist.

I was the only child of my father and mother just as Anis my cousin, who was my senior by a year, was his parents' only child.

Ever since I was young I had not developed a liking for reading, nor was I keen on games or fond of such hobbies as drawing, painting or writing poetry. (Anis had written a whole poem before completing his third year at the primary school and had read it out on the stage before a large audience at the end-of-year party.) Jumping was what occupied my time during my childhood.

'You have inherited nothing from your father, you oaf,' said my uncle to me the day I had cried. I was short, fair-skinned, with thick eyebrows that joined up above my nose, while my father was of medium height, dark-skinned, and had thin eyebrows.

My mother cried the day my father died, and before my uncle arrived from Cairo Mr Riyad took me on one side and patted me on the back: 'You're the man of the family now. You must pull yourself together so that you can stand by your mother. Stop crying and have confidence in God's boundless mercy. From now on you will be exactly like my own son.'

Our house in Beni Mazar was made up of two storeys, the upper one for living quarters and the lower for my father's clinic—and I had jumped from every one of its windows.

Mr Riyad had had no sons before me and my mother was his first wife.

I lived in my uncle's house for seven years. After the first year I finished my secondary school studies. I did not obtain sufficient marks to allow me to join the College of Medicine and thus fulfil my father's wishes. After long discussions and deliberations between my uncle and my mother (my uncle had not agreed to my father's marriage to my mother, my uncle's wife later informed me), he wanted me to join the Teachers' College so that I might be assured of obtaining a post after graduating and because, being an inspector at the Ministry of Education, he was in a position to use his influence to have me appointed, on graduation, to Cairo. My mother wanted me to go to the English Section of the Faculty of Arts because, first of all, I had completed my preparatory education at St Mark's English Evangelical School for Boys in Assiout; and secondly, so that I would be able to travel abroad in the future.

(My mother had obtained the equivalent of the General Secondary Certificate from St Mark's English Evangelical School for

Girls in Assiout, and as her complexion was fairish and she was in the habit of dyeing her hair blonde, she was often called 'the Westerner'.)

On the day we forwarded my papers to the Teachers' College my uncle said to me: 'Listen to what I have to say, Yusuf, and don't follow the words of your mother "the Westerner".'

During seven years at my uncle's house not much happened. I completed my studies at the Teachers' College, in the Botany and Chemistry Section. After I had graduated my uncle used his influence and I obtained the post of science master at a preparatory school in Cairo.

During my second year at the College Mr Riyad Iskandar signed up to go and work in Algeria. He sold his chemist's shop and went away with my mother. Later, a year after I had graduated, I saw her when she came to visit me. My mother loved me a lot.

Nothing much happened in those years. I was not specially active in any sphere, except perhaps in going off to see certain films. I had got into the habit of staying for a long time on the balcony looking at the Palace trees or being immersed for hours at a time in daydreams. I had not known any girls except for some of those who had worked for my uncle's wife, and then my relationships with them had not gone beyond repairing secretly to where they slept.

I no longer jumped.

Sometimes memories of Beni Mazar would come to me: our house, my father, my mother, the streets or the river, but they would quickly disperse—it was even difficult for me to recall to mind the features of my father or my mother without looking at a picture of them.

Then Dr Anis came back from England. My uncle's wife held a celebration. The ground was strewn with sand and bunting was put up; a fatted calf was slaughtered and gifts distributed among the needy. My uncle published his felicitations in the newspapers, and friends and relatives flocked in so that I saw many members of my family of whom I had not previously known. The peace of the house was changed into an incessant hubbub. Anis returned, tall, smooth-haired, and with ruddy cheeks. He returned with fine, elegant clothes and a Mercedes car. He opened crated boxes and produced presents: This is for you, Father, and this for you, Mother, and this for you, Yusuf; and this is for you, Kamel, and this for you, Mary, and this for you, Nadia, and this for you, Maurice, and this for you, Louis, and this for you, Auntie, and this for you, Cousin. Presents for all the family and for all friends—even for acquaintances and those who had come with them. He opened more crated boxes and produced books by the latest writers and philosophers of the age; records of classical music, foreign music, dance music; and hundreds and hundreds of photos in colour and black-and-white of himself studying, dancing, eating, visiting museums, visiting places of entertainment, visiting friends, of himself sleeping and awake. I was greatly delighted at the return of my cousin: he filled my life with joy—at everything he did and everything he saw.

Dr Anis worked at teaching pure mathematics at Cairo University. He was successful and many of the girl students fell in love with him. My uncle's wife put forward a number of girls as possible wives for him but he refused them all.

'I shall not get married before Yusuf does,' he said to his mother, laughing, as she showed him the picture of a girl from an old and respectable family.

In the same year as he returned from England Dr Anis wrote a book on mathematics, a Lebanese magazine published a long short story by him, and he appeared several times on television and spoke on the radio. (The day of Dr Anis's talk on the radio, my uncle informed me that my father had talked on the radio before I was born, on his return from his studies abroad.)

Before the end of this year, Margaret came from England to visit my cousin. She had yellow hair. My cousin married her.

My uncle held a wedding celebration which lasted for three days and gave his blessing to my cousin's 'Western' wife. I moved to a small flat near to my school in Shubra. Margaret had a white complexion and was of medium height. One day she said to me, laughing: 'I like your looks, Yusuf. The way your eyebrows join up reminds me of the Coptic paintings on the Fayyoum coffins.' That day my uncle and my uncle's wife laughed a great deal.

Seven months I spent in my flat between dreaming and wakefulness before I married. At the end of the seventh month death snatched my cousin away without warning. He was attacked by a sudden sharp pain in the stomach and he went on vomiting for three hours. Blood burst out from his mouth. Coughing up his intestines, he died.

The Conjurer Made Off with the Dish

Naguib Mahfouz

'The time has come for you to be useful,' said my mother to me, and she slipped her hand into her pocket, saying:

'Take this piastre and go off and buy some beans. Don't play on the way and keep away from the cars.'

I took the dish, put on my clogs and went out, humming a tune. Finding a crowd in front of the bean-seller, I waited until I discovered a way through to the marble table.

'A piastre's worth of beans, mister,' I called out in my shrill voice.

He asked me impatiently:

'Beans alone? With oil? With cooking butter?'

I didn't answer and he said to me roughly:

'Make way for someone else.'

I withdrew, overcome by embarrassment and returned home defeated.

'Returning with an empty dish?' my mother shouted at me. 'What did you do—spill the beans or lose the piastre, you naughty boy?'

'Beans alone? With oil? With cooking butter?—you didn't tell me,' I protested.

'You stupid, what do you eat every morning?'

'I don't know.'

'You good-for-nothing, ask him for beans with oil.'

I went off to the man and said:

'A piastre's worth of beans with oil, mister.'

With a frown of impatience he asked:

'Linseed oil? Nut oil? Olive oil?'

I was taken aback and again made no answer:

'Make way for someone else,' he shouted at me.

I returned in a rage to my mother, who called out in astonishment:

'You've come back empty-handed—no beans and no oil.'

'Linseed oil? Nut oil? Olive oil?—you didn't tell me,' I said angrily.

'Beans with oil means beans with linseed oil.'

'How should I know?'

'You're a good-for-nothing and he's a tiresome man—tell him beans with linseed oil.'

'How should I know?'

I went off quickly and called out to the man while still some yards from his shop:

'Beans with linseed oil, mister.'

'Put the piastre on the counter,' he said, plunging the ladle into the pot.

I put my hand into my pocket but didn't find the piastre. I searched round for it anxiously. I turned my pocket inside out but found no trace of it. The man withdrew the ladle empty, saying with disgust:

'You've lost the piastre—you're not a boy to be depended on.'

'I haven't lost it,' I said, looking under my feet and round about me. 'It's been in my pocket all the time.'

'Make way for someone else and don't make trouble.'

I returned to my mother with an empty dish.

'Good grief, you idiot boy!'

'The piastre. . . .'

'What of it?'

'It wasn't in my pocket.'

'Did you buy sweets with it?'

'I swear I didn't.'

'How did you lose it?'

'I don't know.'

'Do you swear by the Koran you didn't buy anything with it?'

'I swear.'

'There's a hole in your pocket.'

'No there isn't.'

'Maybe you gave it to the man the first time or the second.'

'Maybe.'

'Are you sure of nothing?'

'I'm hungry.'

She clapped her hands together in a gesture of resignation.

'Never mind,' she said. 'I'll give you another piastre but I'll take it out of your money-box, and if you come back with an empty dish I'll break your head.'

I went off at a run, dreaming of a delicious breakfast. At the turning leading to the alleyway where the bean-seller was I saw a crowd of children and heard merry, festive sounds. My feet dragged as my heart was pulled towards them. At least let me have a fleeting glance. I slipped in amongst them and found the conjurer looking straight at me. A stupefying joy overwhelmed me; I was completely taken out of myself. With the whole of my being I became involved in the tricks of the rabbits and the eggs, and the snakes and the ropes. When the man came up to collect money, I drew back mumbling, 'I haven't got any money.'

He rushed at me savagely and I escaped only with difficulty. I ran off, my back almost broken by his blow, and yet I was utterly happy as I made my way to the seller of beans.

'Beans with linseed oil for a piastre, mister,' I said.

He went on looking at me without moving, so I repeated my request.

'Give me the dish,' he demanded angrily.

The dish! Where was the dish? Had I dropped it while running? Had the conjurer made off with it?

'Boy, you're out of your mind.'

I turned back, searching along the way for the lost dish. The place where the conjurer had been I found empty, but the voices of children led me to him in a nearby lane. I moved round the circle; when the conjurer spotted me he shouted out threateningly:

'Pay up or you'd better scram.'

'The dish!' I called out despairingly.

'What dish, you little devil?'

'Give me back the dish.'

'Scram or I'll make you into food for snakes.'

He had stolen the dish, yet fearfully I moved away out of sight and wept. Whenever a passer-by asked me why I was crying I would reply:

'The conjurer made off with the dish.'

Through my misery I became aware of a voice saying:

'Come along and watch.'

I looked behind me and saw a peep-show had been set up. I saw dozens of children hurrying towards it and taking it in turns to stand in front of the peep-holes, while the man began making his commentary on the pictures:

'There you've got the gallant knight and the most beautiful of all ladies, Zainat al-Banat.'

Drying my tears, I gazed up in fascination at the box, completely forgetting the conjurer and the dish. Unable to overcome the temptation, I paid over the piastre and stood in front of the peep-hole next to a girl who was standing in front of the other one, and there flowed across our vision enchanting picture stories. When I came back to my own world I realized I had lost both the piastre and the dish, and there was no sign of the conjurer. However, I gave no thought to the loss, so taken up was I with the pictures of chivalry, love and deeds of daring. I forgot my hunger; I forgot the fear of what threatened me back home. I took a few paces back so as to lean against an ancient wall of what had once been a Treasury and the seat of office of the Cadi, and gave myself up wholly to my reveries. For a long while I dreamt of chivalry, of Zainat al-Banat and the ghoul. In my dream I spoke aloud, giving meaning to my words with gestures. Thrusting home the imaginary lance, I said:

'Take that, O ghoul, right in the heart!'

'And he raised Zainat al-Banat up behind him on his horse,' came back a gentle voice.

I looked to my right and saw the young girl who had been beside me at the performance. She was wearing a dirty dress and coloured clogs and was playing with her long plait of hair; in her other hand were the red and white sweets called 'Lady's fleas', which she was leisurely sucking. We exchanged glances and I lost my heart to her.

'Let's sit down and rest,' I said to her.

She appeared to be agreeable to my suggestion, so I took her by the arm and we went through the gateway of the ancient wall and sat down on the step of a stairway that went nowhere, a stairway that rose up until it ended in a platform behind which there could be seen a blue sky and minarets. We sat in silence, side by side. I pressed her hand and we sat on in silence, not knowing what to say. I experienced feelings that were new, strange and obscure. Putting my face close to hers, I breathed in the natural smell of her hair, mingled with an odour of earth, and the fragrance of breath mixed with the aroma of sweets. I kissed her lips. I swallowed my saliva which had taken on a sweetness from the dissolved 'Lady's fleas'. I put my arm round her, without her uttering a word, kissing her cheek and lips. Her lips grew still as they received the kiss, then went back to sucking at the sweets. At last she decided we should get up. I seized her arm anxiously.

'Sit down,' I said.

'I'm going,' she said simply.

'Where to?' I asked irritably.

'To the midwife Umm Ali,' and she pointed to a house at the bottom of which was a small ironing shop.

'Why?'

'To tell her to come quickly.'

'Why?'

'My mother's crying in pain at home. She told me to go to the midwife Umm Ali and to take her along quickly.'

'And you'll come back after that?'

She nodded her head in assent. Her mentioning her mother reminded me of my own and my heart missed a beat. Getting up from the ancient stairway, I made my way back home. I wept out loud, a tried method by which I would defend myself. I expected she would come to me but she did not. I wandered from the kitchen to the bedroom but found no trace of her. Where had my mother gone? When would she return? I was bored with being in the empty house. An idea occurred to me: I took a dish from the kitchen and a piastre from my savings and went off immediately to the seller of beans. I found him asleep on a bench outside the shop, his face covered over by his arm. The pots of beans had vanished and the long-necked bottles of oil had been put back on the shelf and the marble top washed down.

'Mister,' I whispered, approaching.

Hearing nothing but his snoring, I touched his shoulder. He raised his arm in alarm and looked at me through reddened eyes.

'Mister.'

'What do you want?' he asked roughly, becoming aware of my presence and recognizing me.

'A piastre's worth of beans with linseed oil.'

'Eh?'

'I've got the piastre and I've got the dish.'

'You're crazy, boy,' he shouted at me. 'Get out or I'll bash your brains in.'

When I didn't move he pushed me so violently I went sprawling on to my back. I got up painfully, struggling to hold back the crying that was twisting my lips. My hands were clenched, one on the dish and the other on the piastre. I threw him an angry look. I thought about returning with my hopes dashed, but dreams of heroism and valour altered my plan of action. Resolutely, I made a quick decision and with all my strength threw the dish at him. It flew through the air and struck him on the head, while I took to my heels, heedless of everything. I was convinced I'd killed him, just as the knight had killed the ghoul. I didn't stop running till I was near the ancient wall. Panting, I looked behind me but saw no signs of any pursuit. I stopped to get my breath back, then asked myself what I should do now that the second dish was lost? Something warned me not to return home directly, and soon I had given myself over to a wave of indifference that bore me off where it willed. It meant a beating, neither more nor less, on my return, so let me put it off for a time. Here was the piastre in my hand and I could have some sort of enjoyment with it before being punished. I decided to pretend I had forgotten my having done wrong—but where was the conjurer, where was the peep-show? I looked everywhere for them but to no avail.

Worn out by this fruitless searching, I went off to the ancient stairway to keep my appointment. I sat down to wait, imagining to myself the meeting. I yearned for another kiss redolent with the fragrance of sweets. I admitted to myself that the little girl had given me sensations I had never experienced before. As I waited and dreamed, a whispering sound came to me from faraway behind me. I climbed the stairs cautiously and at the final landing I lay down flat on my face in order to see what was behind it, without anyone being able to spot me. I saw some ruins surrounded by a high wall, the last of what remained of the Treasury and the Chief Cadi's house. Directly under the stairs sat a man and a woman, and it was from them that the whispering came. The man looked like a tramp; the woman like one of those gypsies that tend sheep. An inner voice told me that their meeting was similar to the one I had had. Their lips and eyes revealed this, but they showed astonishing expertise in the extraordinary things they did. My gaze became rooted upon them with curiosity, surprise, pleasure, and a certain amount of disquiet. At last they sat down side by side, neither of them taking any notice of the other. After quite a while the man said:

'The money!'

'You're never satisfied,' she said irritably.

Spitting on the ground, he said: 'You're crazy.'

'You're a thief.'

He slapped her hard with the back of his hand, and she gathered up a handful of earth and threw it in his face. Then he sprang at her, fastening his fingers on her windpipe. In vain she gathered all her strength to escape from his grip. Her voice failed her, her eyes bulged out of their sockets, while her feet struck out at the air. In dumb terror I stared at the scene till I saw a thread of blood trickling down from her nose. A scream escaped from my mouth. Before the man raised his head, I had crawled backwards; descending the stairs at a jump, I raced off like mad to wherever my legs might carry me. I didn't stop running till I was out of breath. Gasping for breath, I was quite unaware of my whereabouts, but when I came to myself I found I was under a raised vault at the middle of a crossroads. I had never set foot there before and had no idea of where I was in relation to our quarter. On both sides sat sightless beggars, and crossing it from all directions were people who paid attention to no one. In terror I realized I had lost my way and that countless difficulties lay in wait for me before I would find my way home. Should I resort to asking one of the passers-by to direct me? What, though, would happen if chance should lead me to a man like the vendor of beans or the tramp of the waste plot? Would a miracle come about whereby I'd see my mother approaching so that I could eagerly hurry towards her? Should I try to make my own way, wandering about till I came across some familiar landmark that would indicate the direction I should take? I told myself that I should be resolute and take a quick decision: the day was passing and soon mysterious darkness would descend.

The Accusation

Suleiman Fayyad

ՓՓՓՓՓՓՓՓՓՓՓՓՓՓՓՓՓՓՓՓՓՓՓՓՓ

Free time

In the morning he awoke from his second snooze. The time was still before noon. He stretched, yawning, lazily rose to his feet, made the bed and opened the window on to the light of day. The calls of vendors and the shrieks of children flowed in. Leaning on the window-sill, he took delight in the blue autumnal sky, the flat roofs of the houses, the windows. From where he was he could see, through an open window on the ground floor of the house opposite, his fellow-student Abdul Wahhab: sitting in semi-darkness, he was painting a portrait of a girl on minutely squared paper, copying from a photograph stuck with a pin to the top of the picture. On the wall behind it were his clothes on a hanger, the nail from which it hung being covered by his turban.

He drew away from the window and left the room. He went down the stairs. Crossing the walled courtyard of the house, he knelt down to wash his face. He dried his face with the end of his gown and sprinkled a few drops of water on his hair, rubbing it with his hands, and went up again to his room. He went through the hall-way door and, standing before the shelf and mirror, began combing his hair. Entering the room, he took off two lids from the remains of yesterday's supper and sat down to his breakfast. He then quenched his thirst with water and wondered what he should do.

He returned to the window and leaned on it. All too soon he was bored by the spectacle: the bright light, the empty roofs, women sitting by the doors picking over rice, blowing away the particles of dirt, the calling of vendors, the shrieks of children.

He left the window and gazed about him in the room, searching for something to entertain him, to keep him occupied. His school books were ranged along the floor on an old newspaper. Beside

68

them were the books of his colleague and a number of literary books by al-Rafi'i, al-Manfaluti, al-Zayyat, and Ali Adham, also some numbers of the magazine *al-Risala*. He felt no desire to read any of the prescribed books. Of the other books and magazines, he had finished reading the last of them yesterday by the dim light of the lamp. His mind was a blank, incapable at present of giving itself over either to past memories or to daydreaming.

What, then, should he do? He thought about the cafés, about visiting fellow-students who occupied rooms scattered about the quarter. He told himself that today was Friday, the time noon. The cafés would be almost empty of customers and his fellow-students would be busy preparing, on their stoves, the lunches they had bought themselves in the market. He would not find himself welcome. He wished he could go to sleep again; he wished his fellow-student Farag would come back quickly from his trip to the village and bring back with him some of the tasty country foods, some of its fruits, its news, stories about who had married and who had died and who had quarrelled. His eye happened to alight on his turban and that of his fellow-student hanging on their nails. He saw the two pure white, newly washed shawls. Here, he thought, was something he could do. He felt animated, full of enthusiasm.

He brought the two shawls and, one after the other, sprinkled them with water and rolled them up beside him on the bed so that the moist dampness of the drops of water would work its way into the whole of the fine, soft threads.

He brought the two turbans and began brushing the dust from them, restoring to the dark red plush its normal brilliance and splendour.

He took hold of one of the shawls and spread it out fully. Drawing it tight from each direction, he smoothed out its silken creases with the palm of his hand. He pulled it from opposite ends and made a triangle of it. He folded the head of the triangle over on to its base, then again, drew up his leg to his thigh, and fitted it on his knee.

Lifting the end of the sheet on the bed, he extracted several pins from the mattress by their tiny heads and placed them in his mouth; he held them between his lips, the heads facing his teeth and tongue.

He combed through the black tassel with his hand, making sure its silken plaited strands were smoothed out into a single tidy line. The tassel lay towards his chest. Placing the end of the shawl by the corner of the tarboosh opposite the tassel, he began going round it leftwards, the shawl held taut by the thumb of his right hand, gently and precisely until the tip of the beginning had been hidden under the winding of the shawl. The fingers of his left hand began smoothing out the wrinkles and making the fringe show near the end, standing up straight and neat. Then he began putting the pins in with great dexterity: one he put in from top to bottom, a second sideways, while a third he inserted from below, then turned round upwards and pressed downwards.

Finally, he concealed the end of the shawl between itself and the tarboosh in the right-hand corner so that when the tassel was standing upright on the head it would be in line with the neck and back. He then made fast the final movement with three pins, the very number he had estimated from the start. Using spittle, he paid yet more attention to the fringes till they were like needles.

He removed the turban from his knee, put his left hand inside it and twirled it round his left index finger with his right hand. It went round twice, spinning evenly. He smiled at it, at his skill which so few people could equal. Placing it alongside him gently and cautiously, he began doing the other turban.

Having finished both turbans, he placed them carefully alongside each other on top of the books. He covered them over with an old shawl to protect them from invisible specks of dust. Wiping away beads of sweat from his forehead, he seated himself on the edge of the bed.

What should he do now? he thought again. He got up and brought the short-handled palm-fibre broom and began sweeping out the bedroom and hallway. He went downstairs and washed up yesterday's plates. He wiped the sweat from his face with the end of his indoor gown, with its black, red and white stripes, then leaned on the window-sill, hoping to find a fresh breeze, but there was none. The feeling of loneliness came back to him, with its boring, weary emptiness. He thought about his favourite pastime: the dagger and the target.

On the cinema screen stands the girl, her back to the wall. The man with the dagger, when aiming at the wooden wall right behind her, takes hold of the tip of the dagger, its handle pointing downwards, brings it up to the top of his chest and hurls it. It plunges into the wood above her head, perhaps severing a stray hair. The daggers follow in quick succession from his hand until her head, shoulders and arms are all ringed round. The girl leaves her place, the daggers remaining in the wall, and there is applause for this dangerous act successfully accomplished.

From behind the window the villain comes into view: a secret agent or spy, a hired killer. He forces the point of the dagger between the two halves of the window. The sounds of the party spill out. He looks around for the man who is fated to die by his hand. He spots him. Quickly he hurls the dagger with the same unerring accuracy. The poisoned dagger plunges into its target. A loud scream, then silence. The villain who has thrown the dagger disappears and the window remains empty before appalled eyes.

He brought out a knife. Its blade was of black, unwrought, inflexible steel. Its wooden handle was light and out of balance with the heavy blade. It would not work for knife-throwing. He went into the hallway and slammed the door. He tried it out. His assumption was confirmed: the knife fell to the ground. Then he took it by the handle and hurled it. It fell. He retrieved it. He went a couple of steps nearer to the door and hurled it. It plunged into the door, ripping the long fibres. With difficulty he wrenched it out; its tip had gone through to the other side.

He came to the conclusion that this knife caused too much damage, so he returned it to its place in the bedroom and brought the brass pair of compasses. He opened them as wide as they would go. They had a strong, sharp, tapered point. The grooved wheel on the other side, which opened up and held the pencil, was stiff, as was the arm where the place for the pencil was. It would work— he had tried it before—for knife-throwing.

Holding the pair of compasses by the tip, he brought them up and threw them. They plunged into the door. The whole of the point penetrated into the door. He should have stood a little farther away.

He went to retrieve them. Getting them out was a troublesome job. The point snapped off. The main body of the pair of compasses remained in his hand, which had struck back against his chest. He regretted what he had done. He spat at the door and flung the pair of compasses from the bedroom window into the street.

He brought a stone from the courtyard and went on knocking the end of the point from the outer side of the hallway door till it was even with the wood and its other end stuck out inwards. He tried to extract it with his teeth but failed. He knocked at it with the knife till he had flattened it against the wood of the door. Once again he went back to leaning on the window, panting and in a state of angry dejection.

The Visit

As he was returning from the mosque he felt himself as light as a bird, as empty as a strip of bamboo. Traces of dust still lay on the palms of his hands and there was matting on the centre of his forehead. He thought about what the person giving the Friday sermon had said in his first sermon. He tried to remember, but the monotonous voice in which the second sermon had been recited, memorized by heart from far east to far west, chased away every word contained in the first. He thought: Perhaps it has settled in my soul. He assured himself: The important thing is to live in innocence, without spite or malice or envy, 'cleansed of heart' as the Prophet Mohamed had said. The priests of Ancient Egypt had also said nothing but this. Zarathustra, Buddha, Christ. What, then, was the difference between them? All say to you: Do not be wrong-doing. Wronged against? There is no harm in being wronged against. Christ said: 'Turn the other cheek.' Allah said to Mohamed: 'He who attacks you, attack him.' But He also said: 'He who desists and makes amends, his reward is with Allah. Do not act wrongly.' There is no objection to being acted wrongly against. He told himself that tomorrow he would ask his Sheikh at the Institute.

Nearing his home, he again thought: What could he perhaps do? In the afternoon Farag would come. Until the afternoon he should not eat, for he had slept a lot last night and into the morning. He thought about Hindawi's visit. He thought that such a person would not stay alone in his room; every moment he must be doing something. He was vicious, ever-rebellious, ever-irate, with a vitality that was inexhaustible. His sarcasm was never-ending; his eyes gleamed with ill-temper. He had never seen him calm from the time he had first known him. He was in the class at the Institute when the Sheikh was giving a lesson on grammar, on the verb

Kana and its cognates, devoting himself whole-heartedly to it. He had put one of the students as a guard by the door. The guard would shut the door on him, then open it as the Sheikh said:

'Open the door for *Kana* that he may enter.'

The guard opened the door. The student *Kana* entered.

'What do you do?'

'I make the subject go into the nominative case and the predicate into the accusative.'

'O *Amsa,* enter. O *Zalla,* O *Bata,* O *Asbaha.*'

Hindawi's turn came. He entered and gave his answer.

'Give an example,' demanded the Sheikh.

'Hindawi continued[1] running,' shouted Hindawi.

The class laughed at the mention of his name in the example. The Sheikh flew into a rage so as to quieten the class. Suddenly Hindawi began leaping over the desks, returning to his own by an unfamiliar route. The Sheikh screamed curses at him, rushing after him to hit him, but he did not catch up with him.

'Make way, boy,' yelled Hindawi as he jumped.

As Hindawi's feet approached, the boys ducked. The Sheikh was running up and down the aisle between the desks, but Hindawi was always at the other end. He would run after him, beating about with his stick to land him a blow. The stick, though, always caught someone other than Hindawi. Eventually the Sheikh was panting and gasping for breath, puce in the face. He coughed because of the asthma he was always on his guard against. He coughed and coughed till the tears ran down from his eyes, while he cursed the young generation, present times, and the end of the world which was at hand.

He turned off at the street junction to Hindawi's house. He was aware that he was drawn to him by the magic of his biting viciousness, which was both delightful and hurtful. He passed in front of one house, then two more on the right, keeping the door of Hindawi's house to his left. Finding the door open, he entered the dark narrow hallway. The door of his room to the left being open, he stepped down over the threshold.

He found Hindawi unexpectedly asleep at noon. His snoring indicated he had been asleep for some time. The smell of his sweat filled the room with a fecund, nauseating stench. His crinkly hair

[1] The word in Arabic is another of *Kana*' cognates.

was rumpled from tossing about in his sleep. He was sleeping in his woollen galabia with the country-style neck-opening and his silk, striped waistcoat. His Upper Egyptian face was dark brown, sharp-featured, with thick moustache and eyebrows. As he regarded him he thought: if he were not a student he would be a railway porter, a night prowler on village farms, a crooked merchant.

It occurred to him that the other's world was closed to him, that he had never entered it. He would have liked to wake him up, to talk to him. He was on the point of doing so. He hesitated: sleep has its own sanctity, is a temporary respite.

He saw the end of his wallet protruding from his waistcoat pocket through the opening in his gown, as though about to fall, as though some hand had been pulling it out, had then hesitated or changed its mind suddenly. He approached it: its thick leather was dark brown and it bulged with the pieces of paper it carried. God alone—and its owner—knew what good things and secrets it had hidden inside it. He thought of stretching out his hand and seeing what was in it. He thought of taking a small note from the money it contained. He stretched out his hand and touched it. For a fleeting moment his hand stopped there, while his heart thumped. A fleeting moment, no more. This isn't taking, it's stealing. He did not have the right to spy on someone's personal affairs. He pushed the wallet down, covering it over carefully, cautiously, with the end of the opening of the gown decorated with black thread.

As he was walking round the room away from Hindawi, it seemed to him that he saw two half-open eyes, so slightly open as to be scarcely perceptible, fluttering to the suddenly calm rhythm of his breathing. He stared at him for a moment. His breathing was once again heavy and laboured. He reckoned he was completely asleep, now that his eyes were again closed tight. He felt a tenderness towards the sleeping man, a sympathy and affection.

The two wooden halves of the window were open. He closed them gently, taking care to make no noise. He walked on tip-toe. Taking a light coverlet, he covered him up to the chest with it. He arranged the end of the sheet of his own camp bed. On an ash-tray he saw a packet of Gold Flake. He opened it. He felt a desire for a cigarette, to smoke it at his leisure. He took one. He remembered he had some matches at home. He withdrew from the room, stepping over the threshold and up into the hallway. He drew the door to behind him.

As he was leaving the room he saw the landlady sitting in the darkness in another small, narrow hallway, watching him with half-closed eyes. Momentarily uneasy, he left the house.

The Trial

When he awoke to the call of the high-pitched, sarcastic nasal voice, and the movements of Farag's hands shaking him, it was evening. A bewildering surprise was in wait for him: Hindawi was sitting, a short cane in his hand and his elbows resting on his knees, in the only chair in the room. On his face was a scowling, glowering silence and a gaze that was directed towards him with impatient hate. Farag was standing up, with his fair, oval face, his huge nose, narrow forehead and differently coloured eyes; his woollen peasant skull-cap, the colour of cooking butter, was tilted backwards, pressed down upon light, honey-coloured hair, the ends of which showed on his forehead in a triangle; his ears were as large as those of a basket. He rose to his feet, then sat down again. His inner self told him that something unpleasant was going to happen. The light from the fully opened room looked yellow, mournful and depressing. He felt a sensation of sadness and anxiety for which he knew no reason. He reckoned he was ill. Without wanting to, he smiled at Farag:

'Thanks be to Allah for your safe return. When did you arrive?'

'What safety does someone like you give?' the other yelled with nasal sarcasm.

He looked at Farag once, at Hindawi once. He was sure about the unpleasantness. He got to his feet. He was surprised at not finding a newspaper spread out as was usual whenever Farag came back from a trip, with dishes of stuffed vegetables and pigeons on it, and baked eggs and loaves of bread that were still hot, retaining the smell of the oven, of burning and fire. Farag's hand was inside the left-hand opening of his gown, by his pelvis, idly playing.

He went to the window. He looked out, to his left, at the far horizon, broken by lines of roofs. A twilight cloud was reddened by the rays of the facing sun. A thought leapt into his head: Hindawi has been robbed; Hindawi has come to accuse me of the theft.

At the very moment he turned, tense and uneasy, angry and challenging, Farag pulled him by the shoulder. Except for anger there was no other emotion on his face: he had been accused, his punishment had been determined, and nothing remained but the formalities. Despite himself he made the mistake of asking:

'What's happened?'

Hindawi got up with explosive laughter. Putting the stick under his arm, he brought the palms of his hands together. He guessed Hindawi was thinking of the saying: He kills and walks in the murdered man's funeral.

'That's really great, man.'

'What's happened?'

'Hand over the wallet.'

'Wallet? What wallet?'

It was just what he had expected. He told himself that he must be careful. Any word would be held against him.

'What wallet?' he repeated hotly. 'I don't understand. What's happened?'

'Hand over the money. It doesn't matter about the wallet.'

'Farag, I don't understand.'

Hindawi sprang at him and got hold of him by his gown, at the chest, with both hands. Shaking him, he screamed:

'Hand over the money—a hundred and thirty piastres. I'm not the person to be cheated or robbed.'

He stammered, shrinking into himself. Hindawi was twice his size and stronger than ten like him. Farag was six school years ahead of him. Even if he was capable of putting up a fight, what would be the point? He had now become a thief. The matter had been decided and was at an end. He should nevertheless try. Farag had moved him away from himself. He quietened him down, reassured him with a sign from bunched fingers, which also bore a threat.

'Hand over the money,' said Farag, 'and we won't punish you. We'll keep the secret between us as deep down as in a well. No one will know. You're from my village and what brings disgrace upon you brings disgrace upon me. Allah curse the Devil who put you up to it—confess. I'll tell you what: there's no point in confessing, just hand over the money and the matter will be at an end.'

Tears of anger gushed from his eyes.

'I didn't steal,' he screamed. 'Search my belongings, all my books. I took one cigarette from the packet, I took it as a friend.'

'Then you did come into my room while I was asleep,' shouted Hindawi triumphantly. 'He's confessing, Farag.'

'I only took a cigarette,' he said pleadingly. 'Believe me.'

He thought: This too he shouldn't have mentioned. He thought: But the woman had seen him and Hindawi's eyes had been partly open; he had certainly seen him for a fleeting moment.

'You took a cigarette from me?' said Hindawi. 'So you did come to my room. I definitely found a cigarette missing from the packet. Oh yes, he who steals an egg will steal a camel.'

'Hindawi, Sheikh Hindawi, believe me—just the cigarette.'

Farag seated himself on the edge of their two beds that had been brought together under a single mattress. To one side of the room the mattress of his own bed was rolled up and covered with sacking.

'Then we'll hold an interrogation.' He put the question to him: 'Have you any evidence?'

'Evidence? I? Why?'

'Evidence showing you didn't steal.'

'I swear I didn't.'

'Evidence comes after swearing.'

'It is from him I demand evidence to the effect that I stole.' He quoted: 'Evidence is for him who accuses and the oath is for him who denies.'

Hindawi sat himself down in the chair.

'The evidence,' said Farag, 'is that the landlady saw you when you were entering the room and when you left it, and that you admit you stole.'

'Farag, I took . . . as a friend.'

Hindawi laughed. 'Without my knowledge!' he said.

'I thought of you as a friend,' he told himself.

'Don't be annoyed,' said Farag. 'You took a cigarette—from Hindawi's packet.'

'It was on the ashtray,' said Hindawi in affirmation.

'But I didn't steal,' he said desperately—'neither a wallet nor money. I swear. Allah is my witness.'

'So you did take something,' said Farag. 'Confess. Hurry up, I want to change my clothes and for us to get Hindawi his food. We'll bribe him so he'll hide your shame and mine.'

'Farag, I told you, I took nothing but the cigarette.'

'And the landlady?' said Hindawi.

'She's a liar, a liar—she's lying.'

He thought. He remembered. A wallet was sticking out from his pocket as though it was going to fall. A hand was extracting it, was surprised by a step, a push at the door. Fleeing away in haste, the landlady had returned and taken it after he had gone out. Perhaps she had not been there before him. She might, for instance, have gone in after him. His going to Hindawi possibly had given her the opportunity for stealing from Hindawi and then accusing him. He wished he had not admitted taking the cigarette. Up till then it had been possible for him also to deny he had paid Hindawi a visit. Yet his eyes, for a fleeting instant when his breathing had grown calm, had appeared partly open. At that instant Hindawi had seen him. He thought: Why doesn't Hindawi mention this fact now? Maybe he was mistaken about what he had seen. Were this true, he would, by his denial, be more likely to be believed that it was the landlady who was the thief. Her husband was a seller of animal fodder and Hindawi used to sleep with her when he was away.

'Why are you silent? Speak.'

'Hindawi,' he said, earnestly. 'Believe me, I didn't steal either the wallet or the money.'

'Where are they then? Listen—I'll skin you alive.' He turned to Farag. 'I don't want any questioning—he's the thief.'

'Listen, Hindawi,' he said. 'The landlady, your landlady, it's she who stole from you.'

'I've lived in her house for two years and she's never stolen from me, not even when I've been away.'

'But she stole from you this time.'

'Impossible. She's not a thief. She never stole from me before.'

He was on the point of saying something that would cause an explosion but thought better of it. He feared the other's violence, his savage anger. He was somebody who stood up to the Sheikh and the local toughs of the district. Were it not for Farag he would not have been as amenable as he now was.

'There's no point in discussing it,' said Farag to Hindawi. 'I'm hungry and I want to change my clothes. We'll eat first, then. . . .'

'And my money?' Hindawi said to him, his tone reflecting his former composure which he expected and reckoned would be justified.

'You'll get it.'

'How?'

'Listen, Hindawi. Though I've taken nothing from you, I'll pay you the money.'

'And the wallet?'

'I know nothing about it.'

Farag looked amazed. His astonishment passed to Hindawi, who suddenly said:

'I'm demanding back what you took from me.'

'I didn't take anything.'

'Do you think you're doing me a favour?'

'No,' he hastened to say, 'but there's nothing else I can do. You two have pronounced me to be the thief and there's nothing else I can do.'

Hindawi fell silent and his anger increased with his silence. At the same time, though, his mind was on Farag's basket and the food it contained, as Farag took out the dishes from it and spread out a newspaper.

'Wash the plates,' Hindawi said to him.

He carried off the plates and washed them. When he returned he found they were already eating. He saw the pigeons and knew where they were from, the eggs too. In them lay the skill of his mother, the munificence of his father. He wanted to eat. He was held back by shame and having capitulated to what he could not help, to what was inevitable. Farag laughed with delight.

'Sit down,' said Farag in a malicious, tormenting tone. 'It's from your home. Eat.'

He sat down and began to eat. He lowered his eyes to the food, to the movement of his hands. He did not dare raise his eyes.

Ordinarily, they would have been laughing: they would have made jokes and he would have listened and laughed. Unable to resist the desire, he stole a glance at them. He saw their eyes speaking, the sparkle in them charged with warning. Deep within his head he saw the world's light as a sickly yellow, the horizon drowning, during the few instants preceding sunset, in the redness of blood.

The Punishment

He returned from below, having washed up the plates. He entered the room and put them down. He bent down to dry them. He heard:

'Take it—here's your money.'

The voice added: 'He'll have seventy piastres left. His monthly messing is forty and the rest he'll have for himself.'

He thought about the school-book he had to buy for fifty piastres and the price of the cigarettes he used to smoke on the quiet from time to time. He assured himself that his father would believe him. He would tell him what had happened. His father would send him what he wanted—but if he did not question his story he would come and take him away from sharing digs with Farag. As though talking to himself, he said to the others out loud:

'I'll ask my father for a pound. He'll send it.'

He turned to them nonchalantly. This confident gesture set off and precipitated the moment that had been planned. Farag gave the signal to Hindawi with a wink. Farag's father worked as a servant with the village *omdah*. His own father was a teacher, well provided for, a man of position and influence in the village. Hindawi was offended by having the sum of money handed over to him. Perhaps he too had doubts about his having stolen it from him. Hindawi leapt at him. The metal dish fell from his hand and spun round and round before coming to rest, while Hindawi threw him to the ground on his face and seated himself with his full weight on his back, his own back towards his head. Hindawi savagely twisted up his legs, grasping each foot in a powerful grip.

It was as though some sudden catastrophe had befallen him. He did not utter. Not a muscle stirred in resistance. Farag rained down blows with Hindawi's thick, solid yet supple stick on the soles of his feet that had been brought close together. He struggled, with desperate movements of his legs, against the powerful grip on them in an attempt to stop the stick from falling on the veins of the soles of his feet. In a fearful inner silence his tears flowed. He wanted to scream out in protest, in assurance, in entreaty. He made up his mind not to do so. His younger brother never did so when his father was angry with him. He would not say 'Ow', though he knew what the result would be: further blows until he did say it, this placating 'Ow' that brings deliverance. He abandoned his resolution. He moaned. A few more blows rained down, then the beating stopped without a word. Hindawi rose to his feet, picked up the stick, and examined its end which had split and become frayed. He immediately left the room.

Getting up, he tried to stand on his feet. They hurt him. He shuffled across to his own mattress in the corner. He sat down on its sacking. He hid his face between his forearm and upper arm. His resistance collapsed into sudden, hysterical weeping. He heard, through his weeping, the laboured breathing of Farag, tired from the beating he had given him and seated relaxing on the edge of the bed. He sensed that darkness was on the march, that the sun was dropping behind the horizon, the blood-redness tarnished by black night. He sensed Farag's movements, heard them, anticipated them. Farag got up and took off his clothes, changing them for his house gown which was on the clothes-hanger.

The pain had stopped but the swelling in his feet remained. He pressed down on them so as to be able, though with the utmost difficulty, to walk. Scowling, he dried his tears. He thought. He found no word on his lips, discovered no course of action in his head. He sat down again, gravely silent. It came to his mind that as he was taking the cigarette he had had a sensation of stealing. The sensation had flowed out from the tips of his fingers to the wallet, to the waistcoat, to Hindawi, and thus it was that he had looked as though he had had his eyes half open. The sensation had flowed out into the air of the room. It had transmitted itself to the landlady, and she had come along after him and had stolen, as the saying goes, the camel and its load.

But you, Farag, what has all this got to do with you? Your father and mine are the reason. Were this not so you would not have sided with Hindawi against me. It's who your father is, and who's mine. Or is it that you're as frightened of Hindawi's vicious nature as I am?

Raising his head, he looked at Farag. He was sitting with his shoulders and back supported against the edge of the bed. He was smoking with greedy enjoyment and eyeing him with a sly smile. He belched contentedly.

Everything he saw depressed him. Making an effort, he got to his feet and walked in the direction of the corner where the books and turbans were. He threw aside the old shawl and began to demolish Farag's turban. First of all he unwound it, then removed the tarboosh from the middle of the shawl, and then the pins; he even straightened out the special folds in the shawl.

Farag laughed:

'So what. . . .'

He answered not a word, so Farag added:

'You'll do it up again by yourself.'

'Never. It won't happen.'

Farag laughed. 'We'll see,' he stated.

He turned his back so as to sleep for a while. He remained alone, isolated, humiliated to his very marrow. He went and stood by the window, watching flocks of pigeons circling in the air and fluttering their wings in formations that danced, formations of farewell to the light of day.

A Place Under the Dome

Abdul Rahman Fahmy

@@@@@@@@@@@@@@@@@@@@@@@@@@@@@

I got to know him when I was working at the Municipality of Kafr
Dawwar. At that time I was a bachelor and divided my day between
working at the Municipality and sitting in the station buffet. At
first glance he didn't attract my notice for he was one of those Sufi
Sheikhs with a green turban, a gown made up of all the seven colours
of the spectrum and a long, whittled stick, a man in no way different
from other dervishes except for his excessive shabbiness and his dis-
regard for the dirt stains on his gown and his white matted beard
that had never been trimmed or combed.

I was sitting in the café the first time I saw him. He stood in
front of me for a long time, then pointed his stick at me.

'Don't trouble yourself,' he shouted at me. 'It's no use.'

On looking at him I immediately realized that I was in front of a
man who was living in a different world from mine and that his
conversation should not be taken too seriously.

'What's no use?'

'The matter you're troubling yourself about. I'm telling you it's
no use. Leave things to Allah and get me a glass of cinnamon.'

He threw himself into the chair on the opposite side of the table,
and leaning his stick against his thigh, began mumbling things to
himself which I couldn't make out but which I took to be verses
from the Koran. I clapped my hands and Abduh the waiter hurried
across and I ordered the cinnamon.

'For Sheikh Sabir?' he asked, pointing at the man sitting with
me.

Before I could answer Sheikh Sabir had shouted:

'Yes, for Sheikh Sabir—a fiery cinnamon with Sidi Utaiti's
blessings.'

When Abduh brought the cinnamon Sheikh Sabir sipped at it

with a noise that roared in the ears of everyone sitting in the café, then he rose hastily to his feet and hurried off, shouting:

'Sidi Utaiti—my beloved, my quest!'

He hadn't thought of thanking me for the cinnamon or even of saying goodbye.

'Do you know him?' I asked Abduh the waiter.

'That's Sidi Utaiti's beloved. Haven't you see him before?'

He then related to me his story.

No one in the town knew where he'd come from. They had woken up one day to find him amongst them, having taken Sidi Utaiti's tomb as his home. This particular tomb lay on the outskirts of the town amidst surrounding fields; it was a small domed shrine in a state of dilapidation, several of the stones having fallen from its walls and its wooden window having been smashed so that it lay on the ground under the opening. No one thought of renovating it until one morning Sheikh Sabir appeared. He began doing up the tumble-down walls, replaced the wooden window and repaired the cracked door, then he went off to the house of one of the rich merchants and rapped on his door with his stick.

'O you who are rich,' he shouted at him, 'Allah is richer than you. Don't set yourself up falsely against Allah—and send a mat to Sidi Utaiti's shrine.'

In this way he was able to spread mats on the ground round the tomb and to get himself a kerosene lamp with which to light the place at night. Then he took up residence alongside the tomb where he would spend the night praying and holding discourse with Sidi Utaiti in a voice that could be heard out in the road. When morning came he would wander through the streets of Kafr Dawwar uttering the name of Allah and calling upon Sidi Utaiti.

I used to see him from time to time. Sometimes he would ask me for a glass of cinnamon, at others he would refuse it if I offered, but always he would seat himself in the chair opposite me, across the table, and speak disjointedly of things I did not understand. Then, one day, he stood in front of me, pointed his stick at me, and shouted:

'Why are you annoying your father? Go and make it up with him and kiss his hand.'

My father having died several years before, I said to him:

'And from whom did you learn I had annoyed my father? Did he tell you?'

'Sidi Utaiti told me. He came to me in a dream and said to me: "Sabir, go and advise your café friend that he should make it up with his father."'

'I myself can't go to him. Let Sidi Utaiti give him my greetings. When will you be seeing him?'

'When will I be seeing him?' he shouted angrily. 'Every night he's with me—I perform the dawn prayer behind him. O my beloved, my quest, O Sidi Utaiti. Come on—get me the cinnamon.'

Then he threw himself into the chair and began muttering verses from the Koran.

'Have you known Sidi Utaiti long?' I asked him as he sipped at his cinnamon.

'I'm his servant, his slave. O Sidi Utaiti. O . . .'

'And who,' I interrupted him, 'gave you the job of being his servant?'

'He—my beloved and my master.'

Then, taking a reverberating sip from his glass of cinnamon, he went on:

'I was living like you—one of the dogs of this world. I was preoccupied with my belly until Sidi Utaiti came to me in a dream and said: "O Sabir, have shame and turn to Allah in repentance. Come to my sanctuary, I want you." And he began to rain down blows on me, and when I awoke I found that his stick had left marks on my shoulders. I gave up the world and all it contains and came to his sanctuary. I read the Fatiha[1] for him—O my beloved, O Sidi Utaiti.'

Then, calling out to him, he hurried off.

The days passed and I learnt that a large company in Kafr Dawwar had bought a big tract of land on which to build a club for its employees and Sidi Utaiti's shrine was within it. Seeing Sheikh Sabir one night in the café, I asked:

'Is the company intending to destroy Sidi Utaiti's shrine?'

[1] The short opening chapter of the Koran, equivalent to the Lord's Prayer.

Letting go the glass of cinnamon, he seized his stick and waved it about in the air, shouting:

'Sidi Utaiti's power for good will destroy every slanderous tyrant.'

'But they'll have to destroy the shrine,' I said, 'or at least move it.'

'I'm telling you, Sidi Utaiti is stronger than them—tomorrow you'll see.'

He returned to his cinnamon and when he had finished it he hurried off.

The following days proved that Sidi Utaiti's power for good was in truth 'stronger than them' for the company that was going to build on the land decided to rebuild the shrine and to construct round it a mosque for those employees who wished to perform their prayers.

One night Sheikh Sabir came to me, ordered his cinnamon, and said:

'Do you see Sheikh Utaiti's power for good?'

'That they'll build him a new shrine?'

'The hand of the man who wanted to destroy the shrine became paralysed.'

'Allah's greatness, O Sidi Utaiti.'

'Every time he raised the pick to strike at the wall his hand stayed suspended in the air. Didn't I tell you?'

Two months passed during which Sheikh Sabir supervised the building of the new shrine and the mosque. He would spend his day with the workmen, shouting and calling upon Sidi Utaiti, and at night he would sleep alongside the tomb amongst the piled-up stones, until the building was completed in all its glory: windows of worked iron, the floor of white marble, the walls painted in rich colours and decorated in gold, the broken-down door changed for a fine carved one. The floor was strewn with elegant carpets, while a massive electric chandelier hung from the ceiling, its pure crystal beads sparkling. Sheikh Sabir began wandering through the town's streets calling out at every one:

'Sidi Utaiti's got himself a palace. Sidi Utaiti has become the best holy man in the district. O my beloved, my quest, O Sidi Utaiti!'

The company finished setting up the club and fixed a day for the opening. A party was held in the evening so that people could get to know one another. It lasted till midnight and when Sheikh Sabir went to Sidi Utaiti's shrine to spend the night in prayer as usual, the company's manager was leaving the party with his family and met up with Sheikh Sabir at the front door. Sheikh Sabir endeavoured to pass by him and to make his way through the groups of employees who had gone out to say goodbye to him. The manager's notice was attracted by his shabby, patched clothes and thick, unkempt beard, so he called the doorman and asked:

'Who's that?'

'That's Sidi Utaiti's servant.'

'And who's this Sidi Utaiti?'

'The Sheikh who's inside.'

'And that's the man who's looking after his tomb? Looking as filthy as that?'

'Yes.'

'No. Get rid of him. Tomorrow I'll go to Cairo and bring you another Sheikh who's a bit cleaner-looking.'

And so Sheikh Sabir was turned out of Sidi Utaiti's palace.

When I saw him one night in the café he was sad and glum.

'How did they turn you out of Sidi Utaiti's shrine when it was he who ordered you to be his servant?'

He lowered his stick to the ground and said:

'It's not they who turned me out; it was Sidi Utaiti himself who turned me out.'

'It was he who turned you out?'

'Yes, he came to me at night in a dream and said to me: "I don't want you, Sabir—I've got myself someone better than you."'

There was a ring of grief in his voice that shook me to my depths.

'And what will you do now?' I asked him.

'Your Lord is more powerful than all.'

'Where will you go? With whom will you spend your nights?'

'I'll go off and look around for a Sheikh of my own size, someone whose circumstances are as wretched as mine, seeing as how Sidi Utaiti has become too exalted for us.'

The Country Boy

Yusuf Sibai

This story has four main characters and of these only one is, in all probability, still alive today. Of two of them I can say with certainty that they have departed for the other world, and as to the third the good Lord alone knows what has happened to him.

I know not what has prompted me not to change the names of the characters and so spare myself the trouble of thinking up fictitious names for them; perhaps it is laziness, or maybe the certain knowledge that none of them would be upset if the story were to be published. More than all this is my confidence in these characters, for one of them was my late father, Mohamed Sibai, and I am sure that had God granted him a longer life he would have forestalled me by publishing the story himself, as he did in the weekly *Balāgh* with most of the incidents that happened with the late Sheikh Abdul Rahman Barqouqi. As God did not give him the opportunity of writing it, let me do so on his behalf, and if it is true as they say that the departed see us and are aware of what we do, I dare say he will read it and that his loud guffaws will ring out in the heavens as they did in his lifetime on earth.

The story begins a very long time ago—I am positive it was before 1917, which is to say before I was born—in a bookshop in Ghaith al-Idda Street which joins up Bab al-Khalk with Abdin.

Two men are sitting in the bookshop: the owner and the owner's friend. The first was a religious sheikh with a turban, while the second, my father, was dressed in European style. Both men were well-known literary figures of the time.

I can well imagine my father with his bulky body, broad shoulders and full red face, seated in a cane chair with one leg crossed nonchalantly over the other, as though seated at Shepheard's, and alongside him Sheikh Abdul Rahman on another chair with his flowing *gibba* and elegant *kaftan* over his extremely tall body, and with a face no less pink and white than my father's, also with one leg crossed over the other as he pulled at the mouthpiece of a narghile that gurgled beside him.

The two friends were joined by Sheikh al-Fakk, who was leading his son Imam by the hand.

I do not know very much about Sheikh al-Fakk, but I do know that he was a good God-fearing man, clean-living and extremely pious. He had spent his life in the country, and his son having finished his primary education, he had brought him to Cairo to go to secondary school. Who should Sheikh al-Fakk have recourse to other than those two eminent educationalists and men of letters, Messrs Sibai and Barqouqi, with both of whom he was very friendly?

And so it was that the good man brought his son to Cairo and began asking about his two friends till he ran them down at the bookshop. After the usual exchange of salutations, the man began explaining the purpose of his visit.

'I won't hide from you, Mr Sibai, that I'm frightened about the boy in Cairo. I hear it's all depravity and immorality and I'm afraid the lad's eyes will be opened and he'll be corrupted. I told myself there was no one better than yourselves to look after the lad. I'll leave him in your hands, knowing that it's as if he's in his own home, isn't that so?'

'My dear Sheikh,' the two answered with one voice, 'the lad's like our own son. Relax and don't worry about him.'

'That's just what I told myself—who better to come to than you?'

'You're very kind.'

'God bless you both.'

And so Sheikh al-Fakk took himself off, leaving his son in the care of his two friends.

It remains to introduce the fourth character in the story: Imam al-Fakk.

The reader may well imagine, having learnt that Imam the son of Sheikh al-Fakk, had finished his primary education and that his father was frightened his eyes would be opened to the depravities of Cairo, that he was some naïve young child. Imam, though, was no such thing. At that time primary schoolboys were often as old as the fathers of today, with some of them sprouting beards and moustaches. The student Imam al-Fakk was a hulking man. Though he looked silent and quiet, it was a question of still waters running deep. With closed eyes and lowered head, all shyness and diffidence, he would sit beside his father, oozing innocence, when all the time there wasn't a brothel or hashish den in Tanta he hadn't patronised.

This was the pure, God-fearing, upright and inexperienced son whose father feared would be corrupted by the depravities of Cairo; this was the person entrusted to the care of my father and his friend. Now I happened to know from personal experience that my father did not have the time to see about the bringing up of his own children, let alone other people's, and the same was true of Sheikh Barqouqi.

The first thing this God-fearing young man did was to go off to the headmaster of a national school and strike a bargain with him whereby he took a quarter of the fees in exchange for merely registering him at the school: he wouldn't trouble him with attending, taking books or anything of that sort, all that was required being that the headmaster should register him as a student for a consideration of five pounds. Having registered at the school, Imam al-Fakk then proceeded, with the remainder of the fees, to wreak havoc in Cairo.

Days, weeks and months passed and Imam, as the saying goes, went the whole hog, his fame spreading throughout every brothel and house of ill-repute in the city.

News of what his son was up to began to get back to his father from fellow villagers visiting Cairo. At first the Sheikh would not believe it and thought it was all some plot engineered out of envy. At last, though, his suspicions were aroused and he thought it best to go to Cairo to see for himself the real state of affairs and set his mind at rest.

He descended on his son and confronted him with the accusations and rumours, at which the son closed his eyes and began expressing his grief at the wickedness of people and their love of spreading false rumours and slanderous lies.

The father calmed down a bit and his misgivings lessened. Wishing, however, to do away with all his doubts, he took his son and went off to see Sheikh Barqouqi and Mr Sibai.

Leading his quiet, gentle son by the hand, the Sheikh arrived at the bookshop which was the favourite meeting place of the two worthy men of letters.

'I'll make no secret of it, friends,' began Sheikh al-Fakk after exchanging greetings, 'I've been hearing some very bad things about Imam.'

'Nothing wrong, I hope?'

'I was told his conduct was disgraceful, that he was misbehaving himself all over the place, and that he's not paying the least attention to his lessons or the school—that he's really kicked over the traces.'

Great astonishment was expressed on their side. 'Imam? Who said so, my dear Sheikh? Who could say such things? God forgive us! Imam's like a kitten whose eyes haven't yet opened.'

The kitten whose eyes had not yet opened made himself look even more innocent and self-effacing.

'By God, you'll pay for this, Imam you dog,' said my father to himself, 'putting us in this position.' Then, addressing himself to Imam's father: 'Imam? His conduct disgraceful? Why, with him it's from home to school and straight back home again. He's killing himself with studying and we had to tell him to ease up a bit—isn't that so, Imam?'

Imam lowered his head in agreement.

The two friends began reassuring the father, enumerating Imam's good qualities and holding him up as a paragon of virtue. The Sheikh was duly convinced and hung his head in shame.

'By God, that's just what I said to myself but the way people were talking aroused my suspicions, God curse their fathers.'

'My dear Sheikh, they were jealous of you, envious of you for having such a successful son.'

'Never mind, may God forgive them. The journey was not in vain as I've had the pleasure of seeing you both.'

The Sheikh arose to go, his mind completely at ease, and stretched out his hand to take farewell of his friends. At that very moment, a cart drawn by a donkey and carrying a cargo of women hove into sight. Their voices were raised in song, while one of them, wearing a tarboosh and holding a stick, was standing up in the cart and waggling her belly and hips. The Madame, with her fat, flaccid body and red kerchief, with her *milaya* hanging over the edge of the cart, was beating away on a drum, with the rest of the women clapping in time.

The spectacle could well have passed without incident. There was nothing special about it to attract attention and many such carts had passed by the bookshop. However, calamity struck when one of the women caught sight of our friend Imam standing behind his father, his hand outstretched to bid farewell to Sheikh Barqouqi.

Striking her breast with her hand, the woman called out:

'Tafida girl, isn't that Imam over there?'

'By the Prophet, it looks like him.'

Several voices exclaimed: 'Yes, that's Imam all right.'

'And what,' shouted the Madame, 'brings him amongst all these Sheikhs?'

The women asked the owner of the cart to stop and one of them got off, shouting:

'The good-for-nothing's been owing me twenty piastres for the last month. Hey, man, where's the money?'

After this incident the Sheikh took himself off with his son and neither my father nor Sheikh Barqouqi ever laid eyes on them again.

The Snake

Sonallah Ibrahim

And so the road suddenly made its appearance. It was when the driver slowed the car down, bending apprehensively over the steering-wheel, and continuing to take it up the steep slope, then following the road round as he gave several sharp hoots. There was not a sign of a living creature for tens of kilometres in every direction. No one could expect otherwise in this vast and remote desert, yet the driver had to be on the look-out for the unexpected at every bend or rise.

The doctor held his breath as he gazed out of the window at the rocks, huge as fortresses, that stuck up on every side. The noise inside the car grew less, and died away as all the passengers leaned against the windows, staring out in terror at the vast abyss that fell away right alongside the road. At the bend the car slowed down further until it was almost at a standstill. It continued forward at a crawl. There were several short wooden posts painted in red and black fixed along the edge giving warning of the chasm. Two of these posts were lying on the ground. The car negotiated the bend and the road sloped away in front of the driver, who straightened himself in his seat and let the car creep down without altering speed. There was another bend and again the road turned upwards. The sun shimmered on the huge rocks and their black masses gave one an uneasy feeling.

The doctor turned his head round in order to look at the section of road they had left behind them. Below, the long narrow road stretched out amidst the desert in an endless black ribbon, twisting back on itself, falling and rising in circles. He felt the breath of the passenger sitting behind him striking against the back of his neck in short, successive bursts. Then he heard him mutter in a low voice: 'Eh, it's like a snake.'

It was then that everything began to look like something else. Before that there had been nothing but irritation at the four hours the journey would take to Assiout. At the beginning the road had stretched straight ahead, with the desert spread out to left and right unendingly, no single rise obstructing it. The mountains were no more than faraway lines on the horizon. There was nothing to suggest that the geography of the place would change, for the journey coming had been by night, which had hidden the details of the road, its true nature being revealed only when it began to twist and turn up and down, bending and winding as it thrust snake-like forwards.

No bird, animal, or human was to be seen anywhere. There was nothing but sand and rock, also the posts that followed each other in fleeting succession on the sides of the road, some bearing instructions to the driver, others various numbers, of which the doctor failed to distinguish between those specifying the distance still remaining to Assiout from those indicating the distance already traversed by the car. Another group of objects was more like small tombstones bearing numbers that had been effaced and which resembled the old stone busts of Greek and Roman philosophers, pictures of which appeared in books and magazines.

To the left the poles for the telephone that linked the Oases with Assiout ran with the car. Sometimes the poles were supported by wires fixed into the ground, which in turn were made fast with a blocking of stones so that the violent desert winds should not sweep them away. Sometimes the posts stood erect independent of any wires or fixed only by a solitary wire. The poles were thin trunks of brown wood with a short cross-bar at the top so that they looked like crosses. Hundreds, or rather thousands, of these poles raced past the doctor in a straight line on the left. To him they were more like crosses that had been got ready for refractory rebels to be fastened to. Each to be fastened by the hands, the arms to be affixed to the cross-bar, and a long nail driven into the palm of each hand; the body to be tied to the pole with thick cord so that all the weight should not fall on the hands. Blood would ooze from the hands, from the nose, and the mouth. A putrid smell, that drew to it the flies, the vultures, and the wolves would be given out, and the head would loll in dwindling impotence. The eyes, closed yet fluttering from time to time, would give out a bewildered look in whose depths would be accumulated hidden powers that strove to ascertain or comprehend something or other. Perhaps the lips would move too and flutter like the eyes. But no one would ever know what their owner wanted to say.

Somewhere the doctor had read about the crosses set up by the Romans on one of the roads leading into Rome two thousand years ago and on which they had suspended the bodies of six thousand slaves. Those were slaves who had rebelled, had fought, and been defeated. Their crucified bodies remained for some time a source of pleasure and enjoyment to the free Romans. As for the crosses, it seemed their appetite for blood had remained unappeased ever since: the Romans had taken them to their colonies and even after they themselves had left, others had adopted them. It occurred to the doctor that the crosses had no doubt been placed close together like these poles, and that there were still people who enjoyed the sight of blood and crucifixion. Also there were still slaves who rebelled, fought, and were defeated: like the men who were brought to him when he was a doctor in the prison. They stood in front of him in silence, their heads lowered, their chests and backs bared so that their wounds showed, as though they had just been brought down from off the crosses before the birds of prey should tear them to pieces.

The crosses were racing the car. They put on speed when it did, slowed down as it slowed down. The wires that connected them shook from time to time when the winds blew. But the air had become close. The sun glowed and the driver began to slow down slightly. He was sitting quietly, paying no attention to anything around him. He must inevitably have had a feeling of awful boredom, for what pleasure could there be in going back and forth along this long road where there was no relief from the monotony of the scenery? The telephone poles were the very same: the rocks; the kilometre signs; the two empty resthouses; the lorry halted by the side of the road with its driver curled up asleep on top of it; that solitary tent.

It held no trace of life. It was as though its occupants had suddenly deserted it for some reason, or as though wild beasts had preyed upon them, leaving nothing of them. However, somebody appeared suddenly in the doorway of the tent when the car approached it. He was dressed in soldier's uniform and wore a beret on his head, which he pushed back, and drops of sweat appeared on his face and neck. He opened his tunic revealing a dirty vest. Carrying a small notebook in his hand, he slowly approached the car, which had come to a complete stop. He moved towards the driver's door, his features puckered with annoyance.

The doctor realized that it was a control point. At the doorway of the tent another soldier, carrying a gun in his hand and wearing nothing on his feet, appeared. He stood looking at the car without interest, letting his eyes wander over the windows, doubtless in search of some woman's face with which to moisten the aridity of the desert. The doctor reckoned that there was no one but these two soldiers here. He tried to imagine how they spent their time throughout the long days and nights, and how the two of them got their food. It occurred to him that inevitably they must suffer during the night, for the cold of the desert is as unbearable as its heat. Inevitably, too, they must sleep close together. Perhaps, one night, feeling cold and lonely, one of them would cling closely to his companion. For at night—when the cold is intense and the scant coverings are incapable of combating it, and when the sky seems formidable and silent, and the wolves and the wild beasts no one sees are howling—then you know not what may happen.

The doctor was able to perceive the sensation of cold and loneliness in any human being. Maybe the reason for this was that he had spent a large portion of his working life in prisons. In these dark buildings—yellow from outside, murky within—you see everything as normal. When the prisoners used to come to his room for him to examine them, he would regard them with curiosity. They were extremely miserable: sick, aged, and broken. He could not distinguish between them because of their similar blue clothing and expressions of indifference. Some were really sick and had suffered much before reaching him. The others would mobilize all the cunning and guile they possessed to obtain from him a glass of milk, a piece of meat, or a blanket. Yet the doctor could see fear and pain in all their faces.

At the beginning—when he was a young man full of vigour, when everything used to look clear and simple, as the road did this morning before it twisted and turned and tied itself into knots like a snake—he used to think he'd be able to conquer pain. But he was deluding himself, for pain was like cancer—you tear it up by the roots in one place and it immediately makes its appearance in another.

He had reached the point where he used to wake up screaming every night after a dream that never varied. In this dream he would see himself sitting at a small table, his stethoscope hanging round his neck, and behind him a prisoner carrying a container with some red liquid in it which he knew to be blood. After each examination he would immerse his fingers in this container. On both sides of him stood two giants, like guards, in the white garb of nurses: he was dwarfed by them. In front of him were rows of prisoners seated on the ground, but they were not looking at him. Their gaze was directed at one of the giants, who was chewing something between his teeth, while his eyes roved round vacantly and his features looked angry and fierce, giving warning that at any moment he might ragingly return to consciousness. The fat contractor would bring in the milk—which would be drunk by those prisoners who were ill—for the doctor to test it. The man would put the container of milk in front of him on the ground, then pour into it a bucket of dirty washing water. Then another man would enter carrying the carcass of meat from which the prisoners would eat; he would approach him so that he could test it; smilingly he would show him its diseased and lacerated parts, and would then take it off inside. As for him, he would wave his hands and want to shout, protest, refuse, and threaten, but the sound would be imprisoned in his throat and there it would grope about, clawing with its talons at the roof of his mouth.

But it was not possible for this to go on for ever; it was destroying his nerves.

His nerves were calm now. His stomach, though, had begun to be upset by the bumping of the car. For, despite the fact that the road had been built and made up two years ago, the paving had been damaged in many places. The doctor thought that the opening up of the road could not have been a difficult matter, for the desert stretched out like a plain except for one or two places. The car was now approaching one of these uneven places, which was a semi-tunnel in the middle of a mountain on which could be seen the marks of recent work. There was no doubt that hands and machines had cleared this tunnel in the middle of the mountain. The two feet of the mountain, with their red rocks, were very close together. The car proceeded slowly through the tunnel and the whole air became dyed red. The driver again bent over the steering-wheel apprehensively, and the passengers looked out of the windows in terror at the huge rocks suspended over the mountain foot an arm's distance away, as though about to fall at any moment.

The doctor was gazing with curious anticipation at the mountain peak and base as though expecting coloured heads to emerge from them, shrieking, assailing them like locusts, and raining down poisoned arrows upon them as happened in films. Or that shots would suddenly ring out from everywhere, aimed by unknown enemies lying in ambush. It did not occur to the doctor that he was dreaming or imagining things, for he knew that something similar was happening on the other side of the desert across the sea. Perhaps at this very moment there was just such a mountain over there, with red rocks and ravines and caves in which the killers were hiding. Perhaps there was a soldier sitting on the edge of it, while behind him several half-naked men, carrying daggers and knowing nothing about anything except killing, were stealing up upon him. Silently they would fall upon the soldier and stab him all over. He would roll to the ground, his blood leaving a red line behind him: quickly it would congeal, coagulating with the earth. He would roll rapidly, the dust rising above him, until he came to rest at the bottom. Above, the brutish fighting would continue, then stop after victory had been achieved. Reconstruction would begin. Roads would be opened, factories would be built, cinemas put up, and love songs would be composed and broadcast over the radio. The murdered soldier would not hear them. He would see none of all this, for he would never again leave his place in the desert.

In the desert the doctor was travelling on in the car, irritated by the heat and the boredom. His watch told him that the car had covered half the distance. He was thinking that he should have brought a small radio with him to while away the journey. In Cairo people were eating ice-cream and drinking glasses of iced mango juice and watching the television. Again they passed by a lorry that had turned off on to the side of the road, its driver curled up on the back of it fast asleep.

In front of him in the car were sitting two smart young men, one of whom expressed the opinion that the road stretching before them through the sands reminded him of the road to Alexandria. This also was the view of the other who had had some strange experiences on that road when he was going along it in a small car called *Kiki*. Beside the door was sitting a passenger of slender build, huddled in his seat which was over the raised part above the front mudguard, looking dwarfed. He was immersed in his thoughts, as though reckoning up his life. Certainly his thoughts were not heartening. This was not surprising, for when one is in the middle of the desert and one's face is pouring with sweat and the road in front appears to have no end, when thigh muscles ache and nerves have begun to protest, when one is squirming about in one's seat searching for somewhere to be comfortable, when, besides, one has passed forty—then death becomes embodied before one as the finality of everything.

To any doctor death is something familiar, although it sometimes causes one to reflect about it. This was what had happened yesterday: when he was making his tour of the hospital wards in the Oases, depressed by the flies, the heat, and the dust, he had been thinking that death was the fate of everyone, and that no ill person was the worse off if he should die today rather than tomorrow seeing that this was bound to happen one day. This thought was a simple and intriguing one. It meant that he should finish this disagreeable task quickly in order to take himself off to the Governor's air-conditioned room.

This was an easy matter; during the last few years it had been without any importance to him. It was enough to keep the inside of one cold and unmoved in order not to care, for everything to appear plain and easy, and for things to carry on uncomplicatedly. The floor was filthy, the pails of water that had been poured over it hastily to remove the filth having been unsuccessful. The male nurses were clothed in sparkling white uniforms, but he knew they would take them off when he turned his back on them. The sheets covering the beds were clean, but he was able to imagine what was hidden beneath them. Yet all that was of no importance. It was enough that everything appeared all right and that he was able to make his departure immediately.

The sick lay on their beds in clothes that were identical and approximated in colouring to the yellowness of their faces. They were following him with their eyes, but for which he would have supposed them to be corpses devoid of life. From the way they looked at him he realized that he should not give any one of them an opening or he would never get finished. And so he kept to the wing of the main corridor between the beds and avoided meeting the eyes of any of them. He would turn his back on them, raise his eyes to the ceiling, put his hands in his pockets, and incline his head forward so as to gaze at some object on the bare stone floor. But always he felt the eyes fixing themselves upon him: strong and commanding, drawing him despite himself. They would compel him to turn to them, to face them perplexed. The sockets were wide and deep-set, but something strange was gathering itself together in their depths; something that drew and bound and fettered; something ancient and familiar that could not be ignored.

*   *   *

The doctor relaxed in his seat and continued to look out of the window opposite, by the left-hand pane of which sat the driver. He knew that the snake stretched out behind. In front there was nothing. The road did not appear to extend beyond a few paces ahead. The desert concealed it carefully, only revealing it bit by bit. The road would sometimes rise up suddenly, and only a single step ahead was to be seen. The driver would press down on his horn in warning, and when the rise vanished the road would unroll ahead again, completely featureless. The doctor almost smiled at the deception that was incessantly repeated and which each time tricked him. To the rear, the snake could be clearly seen twisting away, leaving its tail far away, way back at the Oases. As for the head, it was creeping forward with feverish speed, craning its neck in yearning impatience to see what was to come. Suddenly the mountains appeared, as though barricading the road. For a moment the doctor wondered where the driver would take himself, how he would get through. But the head of the snake soon pushed its way miraculously through at a place in the vicinity of the mountains.

The road was now free from bumps. The car was racing along quickly and easily. The kilometre number signs followed one another. The doctor was able to solve the puzzle of these numbers now and to tell which indicated the distance that remained and which showed what had been completed. The distance that remained to Assiout was no more than fifty kilometres. Silence reigned in the car. Some of the passengers leaned their heads forward on to the backs of the seats opposite them and had sunk into sleep.

The doctor's irritation had reached its peak. His eyes were tautly focused on the country that undulated through the other side of the window, and at every bend or rise he indulged the hope that after it would appear the houses and buildings of Assiout; but each time he was suddenly confronted by new hills and expanses of sand. The road looked endless. The kilometres seemed to get longer, to come to an end only with great effort—the number forty remaining static for a long time. Finally the doctor decided to refuse to have anything to do with these numbers and not to follow them with either his eyes or his mind, to think of something else with which to occupy the time. It was then that the long dark line appeared.

It stretched far away into the horizon, but was rapidly coming nearer. To begin with it most resembled a heavy cloud in the far sky, then it soon seemed nearer to the earth than to the sky. The doctor turned round slightly to the passenger sitting behind him and asked him his opinion. The latter immediately gave his reply— with a sigh of relief he said: 'Assiout.'

The car was now scarcely touching the ground. A kilometre sign passed and he saw it said thirty. The dark line began, moment by moment, to grow clearer and its dark colour turned to a dense green, which rapidly drew closer, the head of the snake every moment tilting to right and to left with the turnings of the road as it resolutely made its way towards the greenness. The passengers began to lose their lassitude and to rise in their seats as they gazed with interest at the faraway fields. This was the moment when there appeared the large white slabs arranged in sloping rows opposite the fields. The doctor leaned forward as he followed them with his gaze, wondering what they were. After a while he discerned large stone structures, like benches, some of which consisted of several storeys, like the step pyramid of Sakkara. There were not so many of them. They were well-proportioned and the sides were of equal size, the edges polished—or this was how it appeared from afar. Some of them bore lines and naïve patterns in red, like those drawn on the houses of returning pilgrims in the villages or the poorer quarters of the towns, and on which they would scrawl: Pilgrim shriven, sin forgiven.

The doctor fidgeted in his place, perplexed. The passenger sitting behind him, as though conscious of his perplexity, said: 'This is Assiout's cemetery.'

A faint smile traced the doctor's lips, and it occurred to him that he had never seen graves such as these, though he had visited many villages and towns. The car turned to the left, having slowed down, and began to cross a steel bridge. Suddenly people appeared on every side as though the ground had spewed them forth. The peasants began, as was always their way, to inspect the car and its occupants in astonishment. Three young schoolchildren hurried along the side of the bridge, their sleeves rolled up, hugging their books tightly to them. The doctor's gaze followed them with nostalgic sadness. The car crossed the bridge and turned off into a broad street shaded by trees. The Nile waters flowed along on the right, deep and vast.

The journey had not come to an end yet, for there still remained a few kilometres to the town. The snake-like road, however, had disappeared; when the doctor turned round to look he detected not a trace of it. By then it was buried in the sands of the desert. Likewise he could not make out the strange tombs of Assiout, for the tall, bulky, blue gum trees screened everything that lay behind them. The trunks of these trees had begun to take up the race with the car.

The Crush of Life

Yusuf Sharouni

▼▼▼▼▼▼▼▼▼▼▼▼▼▼▼▼▼▼▼▼▼▼▼

I'm a squashed up sort of a person whereas previously—a third of a
century ago when I was an adolescent—I was fat. My father (God
rest his soul) was the same, and my mother remained corpulent till
the last moments of her life. They had spent the early part of their
lives in the country where open spaces gave room for both fat and
thin. As for myself, I was forced, amid the clamorous crush of the
city, to rid myself of my corpulence so that I could both find breathing space for myself and make room for the others.

For twenty minutes I've been standing at the bus stop, trying to
get on a bus so that I can go and start my shift. I'm a bus conductor
with the Inland Transport Company and I've got only twenty
minutes before I'm due to start work. A bus passed but did not
stop: it was replete with passengers and couldn't swallow another
one. A second one came along; this time it stopped and those who
wanted to get off were jammed tight against those trying to get on.
All stood their ground. Finally the bus sorted out a number of arms
and legs and ejected them, and sucked into itself a further number.
I tried to force my way through the battle of those getting off and
those getting on but scarcely had I found room for the toes of my
right foot than the bus moved off. I reeled back, struggling not to
lose my balance, but something struck me violently on the chest and
I fell. I regained my feet and stood in the road brushing the dust
from my clothes.

I am Fathi Abdul Rasoul, bus conductor and poet from the village
of Kom Ghorab, district of al-Wasiti, province of Beni Suef, where
I spent my childhood among the vast fields, with a horizon that
stretched as far as the eye could see. My father used to take part in
the dervish circles of Sheikh Shaarani and would rock his inordi-
nately fat body from side to side, while I watched him with joy and

awe and tried to imitate him. I still recall, at moments like streaks of light, those evenings when, by the dim light of a lamp, he would read the story of Sayyid el-Badawi or the Supplications of Sheikh Mitwalli. Beloved of everyone, he was being proposed as the successor to Sheikh Shaarani; people would reverently kiss his hands and would bend over and kiss me on the cheek with gentle playfulness.

I'm terrified of crowds. I've been frightened of them ever since my father took me with him to the anniversary celebrations of Sidi Ahmed el-Nouti. When he joined in and led the dervish circles, he would completely forget about me. I had wanted to ride on one of the swings and had then stood and gazed in wonder at a sugar horse with a small rider on it of perhaps my own age. Then someone selling paper hats passed by and I followed him for a while until I suddenly felt I was lost in the crowd. I went running anxiously among the circles of dervishes: all resembled my father but none was he. I burst out crying. As I ran, I bumped into people, seeking protection both from them and with them in my terror and panic. Had I been with him in the fields I would have seen him from a distance greater than that occupied by the celebrations. That day the only person to come to my rescue was a man from our village. I heard him say: 'The son of Abdul Rasoul crying? What's wrong, boy?' Then he led me off to my father, and since that day I've been terrified of crowds.

When my father left the country to seek for his livelihood in the big city, I was still an adolescent. The first signs of inherited corpulence had begun to appear on my body. My voice had started to break while I was attending school, where I was learning to scan through the pages of the books my father used to read: *The Diffusion of Scent in Praise of the Beloved Heaven-sent, The Traveller's Provision on the Journey to the Unveiled Vision;* and I was particularly thrilled by the stories contained in the book *The Garden of Herbs Aromatic in the Tales of the Devout and the Ascetic.*

I was overwhelmed by the big city with its hugeness and crush of people: it was as though a thousand anniversary celebrations were going on at one and the same time. It was obvious that we had come too late, for there was no room for any more people. When I saw the towering, multi-storeyed buildings I was amazed how houses could be packed together like this, one on top of the other, and was always frightened that this great weight would bring them toppling down on the people living inside. For the first time I saw trams and buses; they were crammed to overflowing and themselves blocked up the streets of the city. It seemed as though everyone, men and women, young and old, were hurrying towards something, like a flock of jostling sheep on their way back to our village at sunset, each plunging forward to force a way, isolated and alone, amid the crush of people. I was suddenly overcome by a feeling of deep gloom, deeper than that which had overwhelmed me the day I was lost at the anniversary celebrations. If I got lost here and cried, I would find no one to say to me: 'What's wrong, boy?' Here you know no one and no one knows you.

My father managed—maybe through some miracle he worked—to create a job for himself and to find us somewhere to live. The job was a small grocery shop, while our home consisted of a room which housed my mother and father, my young sister Saadiya, and me, also the odds and ends of furniture and books we had brought with us. The room was a semi-basement, its narrow windows barred like a prison cell; the sun reached it only at secondhand and it was as though our day were a perpetual chilly twilight.

The rooms were all packed close together; in them the bodies of men and women clung together tightly when the darkness of night united them, and they bred like rabbits: passions at odds produced noisy quarrels, reciprocated desires set sex ablaze. Shouting was the sole language recognised by the inhabitants of this floor, shouting in which words were not important: it was as though vast distances separated man from wife, son from father, and a woman from her neighbour.

It seems that the owner of the building, in order to save money, had made our ceiling so low that anyone entering had to bow down; only children were able to come in standing upright. You would see men and women screaming and laughing and moving about doubled up like bows. And so, directly they entered, the first thing they saw was their feet and the ground under their feet. Sleep was their one chance of straightening their bodies again, though in winter, in order to keep warm, they preferred to remain doubled up even when asleep. At first we found this difficult because of our corpulence, though we soon got used to it. The room contained one bed on which my father and mother slept, while my sister and I used to sleep on a mat on the floor.

My mother had given birth six times: three of the children had died in their first year, and a girl before she attained the age of two. Only my sister Saadiya and I had survived. While giving birth for the seventh time my mother died: she had a haemorrhage which the midwife did not know how to cope with. It all began in the evening and was over by morning. That night our neighbours went without sleep. The women gave all the sympathy and help they could: a word of encouragement, a piece of cloth, sighs of distress, a tin basin, a sheet, shrieks. When, in the morning, the men learned that all was over, they proffered what money they could collect together as a loan to my father to help with the funeral expenses. The men who carried her coffin found it a very heavy load—it was said that her excessive corpulence contributed to her early death. My father mourned her, my sister mourned her, and I mourned her.

A month after her death there was a bride in our room occupying my mother's place in the bed.

Awatef was no stranger to us. After living in a nearby room she and her family had moved to a less expensive one in a neighbouring quarter. She was twenty years of age and my father was getting on for fifty. While I received her first of all with a certain amount of reserve, she did her best to be friendly to my sister and me; her prettiness, too, helped to do away with any antagonism on my part. Within a few weeks she had convinced us that life could not continue in our room without her. During the month following my mother's death things got badly out of hand: while the neighbours would wash our clothes for us and my father would buy food from the market, the room itself became piled up with dirt. When Awatef came, everything became organized again; in fact the room looked tidier than in my mother's day.

At that time I had obtained the Preparatory Certificate. My father tried to get me into one of the secondary technical schools but everywhere we were told there was no place: my total grades were not sufficiently high.

My father heard there were still some places in an institute of physical training and entrants were not required to have any set grades. No sooner, though, had the institute's secretary seen me—

and my father too—than he made us understand we were wasting our time.

'We've only one free place,' he said to my father, smilingly regarding my corpulence, 'and your son needs two!'

'But your gymnastics may make him thinner.'

'No, it's up to him first of all to go into training: a slim figure is essential for entrants to our institute.'

I returned home, dragging my corpulence along in embarrassment; I was like some creature that crept or crawled. I had breasts like a woman's, like the udders of a milk-cow in Kom Ghorab, while the flesh of my stomach hung down in folds and my buttocks were flabby. From every flaccid fold of my body there oozed a sticky gelatinous sweat.

For a modest subscription I at once joined a club where I began doing strenuous exercises. By the time my body had slimmed down, the date for acceptance had passed and I realized I had no chance of entering a school and had better look round for a job.

To save himself the trouble of trying to find me a job, my father decided to take me into his grocery shop. There being no room for both of us, he sacked the man he employed, accusing him of cheating him over the customers' accounts.

At the beginning of each month people would crowd into the grocery, their grimy ration-cards in one hand, their grimy money in the other. If some commodity had disappeared from the market and word got about that Abdul Rasoul's grocery had some left, they would come along, pushing and hitting out in an effort to get hold, if possible, of the whole quantity. Even when our stock had run out, the people would still be exchanging blows.

At such times my job was to push them away from our shop so that our goods would not come tumbling down on top of them or be filched.

My relationship with my father was one of admiration and awe rather than of affection: I admired his courage and stood in awe of his ruthlessness. Working as he did in the grocery morning and evening, he had given up being a religious leader. Sometimes he would catch me reading, or writing a song, when he would jeer at me: 'Why, then, weren't you any good at school? Why don't you seek to make your living as your family does?' I sent one song after another to the broadcasting station without ever receiving a reply. Keeping it secret from my father, I tried to write songs like those about love and love's torments, though in them I also gave expression to a burning passion that had begun to stir within me.

At night, brought together in our room after the lights had been put out in the nearby rooms, and the piercing shouts had died away and had changed into something resembling whispers, I began to become aware of certain things. In a semi-sleep I would hear mysterious sounds and movements coming from where my father lay with his bride. With a mixture of curiosity, disgust and excitement I gradually began to become aware of what was going on in their world.

In summer I preferred to sleep outside in the hallway which communicated with the rest of the rooms, but in winter I found it too cold there. At the end of the year Awatef gave birth to her first child; it happened at noon.

I have begun to grow bald and the sun's heat scorches my head. The hot weather has wilted the radiance of women, their perfume has evaporated, and the smell of sweat rises from under their armpits. No third bus has come. I ask a man beside me for the time and he snorts: 'A million o'clock!' A woman shifts her child from her right shoulder to her left, then back again, regularly every two minutes. An old man lifts up his eyes and gazes into the sun's disc, then asks me for the number of the approaching bus. From time to time someone, having given up hope, leaves the stop, raises his hand and yells: 'Taxi!' and opens the taxi door.

In the grocer's shop my father raised the knife wanting to stab me:

'What are you doing, you son of a dog? Still writing love songs? Is this all the upbringing I gave you has done! I wanted you to be the Sheikh of a dervish order and all you've become is a Sheikh of depravity!'

The customers intervened: 'Let him be, man—for my sake—all boys are like that.'

'Let me show him, the scoundrel! Even here he's no use!'

Though they managed to snatch the knife from him, he struggled free of the hands that encircled him and slapped me on the side of the face. Several packets of soap toppled down. I thought of hurling one at his head. This was not the first time such things had happened; I was resolved it should be the last.

It was not to be the last. Finding another job took time. Finally a friend took me off to the Inland Transport Company. I stood in front of the employee responsible for receiving applications and was reminded of how I'd stood in front of the secretary of the physical training institute. My corpulence didn't appeal to him either (though much of it had by now vanished).

'Our vehicles are crowded,' said the man, 'I mean overcrowded. We even have passengers your size. How will you squeeze yourself between them? We want conductors as slim as sticks of sugar-cane, while you—you're more like an elephant or a porpoise. Ha ha ha!'

I joined in the man's laughter, anxious not to appear both obese and uncouth.

'Our company,' he continued, 'likes the buses being overcrowded, the more crowded they are the more money it makes. We give our conductors a bonus—eight piastres when the takings reach ten pounds and four piastres for every pound after that. Your body will prevent you getting any sort of bonus.'

'I promise you,' I implored, 'I'll lose weight.'

'Why do you eat so much? Leave something for the others, old chap! Ha ha ha!'

'Ha ha ha! Don't think I'm a millionaire! I promise you from now on I'll not eat.'

'I'll accept your application, but the main thing is for you to convince the examiners at the interview.'

I returned to the club that sold slimness. There I found dozens of others, each doing strenuous exercises in the hope of losing a little weight and so finding a job or a place in some school. The exercises were torture: bending and straightening, sitting down, standing up, stretching, raising one arm and lowering the other, twisting to right and left, arching backwards and forwards, all as though in a circle of dervishes, until the sweat poured out of me and I was panting like a dog being chased by some wild animal.

I drank less water, denied myself a siesta, and confined myself to a single meal a day. As though it were some frolicsome horse, I was breaking in my body in the hope it would lead me through the crush of life.

Though I never attained the shape of a stick of sugar-cane, I was able to satisfy my examiners on the day of my interview. I sang them, to borrowed tunes, some of the songs I had written. One of them laughed, another smiled—it was the first time anyone had shown any appreciation of my songs. And so I became a conductor with the Inland Transport Company.

In the crush of the bus I thought myself to be in one of our ground-floor rooms. The roof was as low as our ceiling, while the people were packed together, all doubled up like bows, just as at home. The bodies of men and the bodies of women were squeezed together and sex was set ablaze. Those getting on collided with those getting off, some treading on others, and noisy quarrels would break out. Someone concentrates his whole mind on a seat that may have been vacated and it becomes for him the most important thing in the world, as though his very destiny depends on it.

'If you'd just allow me to get by, lady.'

'Go ahead—who's stopping you?'

'How can I? You're blocking my way.'

'Think yourself in the Hilton or something? We're in a bus.'

'It's my fault.'

'Thinks he's in the Hilton: "Allow me to get by," says he.'

'She's not happy about the man paying her no attention. It certainly is his fault.'

'Maybe she's in the mood!'

Laughter all round.

'Oh, my foot! My foot!'

'If we're having to put up with this sort of crush now, what will our children be doing?'

'That's the clever thing about my not marrying.'

'The clever thing about overcrowding is that it cures itself by itself—it so upsets people they don't have children.'

'That's better than plagues, famines and wars.'

'Overcrowding *is* war. Every time I look at my children I'm apprehensive about their future.'

'In a few years there'll only be standing-room on this earth.'

'The funny thing is that overcrowding is the result of medical advances—the fact that doctors are now going into the country districts is a blessing that has given birth to trouble. Who'd believe it?'

'Ah! I banged my head on the roof.'

In the second-class a woman's voice was saying angrily:

'D'you mind moving over.'

'If you don't like the crush, take a taxi.'

'You're rude.'

'It's you who's rude.'

'Take it easy, it's only for a few minutes.'

There were two more minutes to go before I started my shift. My bus will wait for me until it's crammed full of passengers, then they'll shout for the inspector and dock me a day's pay. I can't bear standing any longer: my joints are on fire.

One morning my father complained about his joints, about his right knee to be exact. In the evening he complained about his other knee as well and of being feverish. He poured with sweat that smelled of vinegar. He took an aspirin and went to sleep. In the morning he refused to rest. I said to him: 'Rest, father—Awatef will go to the grocery.' His eyes flashed like those of a wild animal and he shouted: 'I know, you want to come in to all I've got while I'm still alive.'

'Believe me, I just want you to rest, I'm worried about you. In the morning you left with one knee hurting you and when you returned in the evening with both knees . . .'

'You want to sell the shop so as to buy pens and paper,' he shouted, rising up to attack me. 'Awatef is not leaving here!'

As usual the neighbours came along out of curiosity and a desire to intervene. They settled our quarrel.

He went off to work, strong as an ox, ready to do combat with death itself. Then, suddenly, he took to his bed, unable to bear anyone to touch any part of him. His joints swelled and filled with liquid. The doctor said the disease had reached his heart. He was convulsed by coughing and vomiting. Each time he coughed, he felt his intestines being rent—and with them my heart. The look of terror in his eyes was mirrored in my own.

At night, after we had buried him, after the gathering of mourners had broken up, after my sister Saadiya had wept for him and returned to her husband's house, after my half-brothers and sisters from Awatef had wept and gone to bed, Awatef herself was still weeping. While I was unable to shed a single tear, I wept in bitter silence.

I realized that I had in truth come into my father's estate: the young mouths he had left me to feed, what remained of his books and belongings, his shop—and Awatef. I tried to console her and calm her down, though it was I who was in need of being consoled. Her black mourning emphasized her pale complexion: I had not previously noticed how milky white her skin was, or how soft.

On the night following my father's death I discovered she had a beautiful nose. I realized that the nose, being in the centre of the face, determines its beauty or ugliness; thus, if it is unduly long or large or snub, it throws a shadow of ugliness over the surrounding features. Her nose, being delicate, endowed her lips, chin and eyes with such beauty that I wanted to kiss it, to kiss just the tip. All this I wrote down in a song.

At night I dreamed I was carrying my father and that he was groaning in pain. His corpulence made him too heavy for me, particularly as I had now become thinner. I fell down and brought him down with me. I heard him moaning. 'How could you let me fall, cruel and heartless one?' he cried in distress. At that moment I melted with tenderness and compassion for him, seeing his pains increased by reason of me. I woke in a state of alarm and found Awatef asleep in my father's bed, breathing gently. A part of her, more naked, white and soft than I had found it yesterday, was exposed. I approached and gently covered her up. I could feel the warmth she exuded.

The following nights I made a point of not returning early, not until after Awatef had gone to bed. I asked to be put on night-shift, which I preferred as then the buses were slightly less crowded.

On the eve of the fortieth day after my father's death, I had to be alongside Awatef to receive those who came to offer their condolences. That night I discovered what sort of voice she had. I don't know how it was I hadn't discovered this before: her staccato way of speaking was like a call, its huskiness like desire. That night I did not sleep far from her; I was not separated from her by my brothers and sisters but slept directly under her bed. That was at the beginning of the night. In the middle of the night it came about that I found myself sleeping where my father used to sleep. It was then I became aware of her feet, her toes, her toe-nails. We were mad with desire for each other. Then she fell asleep and so did I.

I was at the anniversary celebrations and they were being held in a bus. There was a procession heading towards me, moving nearer and nearer. The crowd was dense. They were saying prayers and incantations and carrying banners and torches and drums. At their head was my father; he was riding a large sugar horse and was wearing a dervish's conical cap and brandishing a sword. The hooves of his horse were trampling over me, his sword striking at me. Behind him the people were shoving one another as they did when taking their rations from the grocery or when trying to board the bus without letting the people off first. They pushed each other and trod over me. I shrieked but no sound came from me, my mouth being filled with dust. I was being crushed under them as they trampled over every bone in my body. My book of tickets was lost, the money in my satchel scattered about. I tried vainly to cling to what was left. Oh, they'll sack me! I have only twenty seconds to go before the time for starting my shift. My whole body still bears the imprints of their shoes and feet, while on my right knee is the wound from my father's sword. My body is steeped in sweat that smells of vinegar. The disease will creep up to my heart.

I am Fathi Abdul Rasoul, bus conductor, poet and lover. We are all in the one room. Her eldest son has begun to notice certain things. He wakes up in the night as though wanting a drink from the water jug. He looks towards us. I have moved away. Perhaps he wants her for himself? I have doubts about his intentions.

'What are you doing, Sa'id?'

'Just having a drink.'

'Having a drink, are you?'

Awatef wakes up.

'It's night,' she says. 'Walls have ears—have some shame!'

'What's this boy up to with you?'

'You mean my son Sa'id? Are you crazy?'

'I'm not crazy. Why does he get up every night?'

'He wants to have a drink or go to the lavatory.'

'I know what he's up to!'

I gave Sa'id a slap on the face. His mother screamed. The neighbours woke up.

'Keep the madman away from me!' Awatef went on screaming. 'Keep the madman away from me!'

At dawn I caught sight of my father in a corner of the room wearing the uniform of one of our company's inspectors. He was sitting cross-legged, swaying to right and left, the daily work-sheet in his hand; it was as if he was chanting from it:

'O cruel, heartless one

I'm your father, forgetful son.'

As though in a circle of dervishes he went on repeating his chanting until I remembered to recite the Fatiha,[1] when he disappeared. Later, though, he came back. At first he would come only at dawn, then his visits increased in number and occurred at all hours.

In the crush of the bus I would be so overcome by fits of depression and fear as I bent over, giving out the tickets, that I lost all desire to go on living. I retained only that minimum amount necessary for persevering with it. I lost my appetite for food and sleep, my feelings for Awatef, even my ability to write songs.

'Your ticket, lady.'

'Just a moment. Ah! My purse—where's my purse?'

'A pickpocket's had it. Thief! Thie . . . eef!'

'Stop the bus!'

'We've got appointments to keep.'

'Search the passengers!'

'A small boy was standing next to her. He jumped off two stops ago.'

'Was there much in it?'

'May God make it up to you, lady.'

While the woman was cursing and blaming the overcrowding, each passenger was feeling around in his pockets.

'How much did you give me?'

'Five piastres.'

'How much change did you get?'

'Nine piastres.'

'And how do you work that one out?!'

'How should I know what a ticket costs in your bus.'

'Ha ha ha! He he he! Ho ho ho!'

I want to take in the smell of greenness, to breathe in the moonlight spread over fields of maize. Nowadays I smell nothing but the stink of sweat and sour breath. At night the moonlight is suffocated by the closely packed houses. They have driven the moon from the city. This was in a song.

Awatef looked after the grocery. She would leave home in the morning and not return till night. More than once I dropped in on her without warning to see if she was flirting with a customer. The shop was more crowded than ever. I found that Sa'id was helping

[1] The short opening chapter of the Koran, equivalent to the Lord's Prayer.

her after he came back from school. She wasn't giving me my share of the earnings. I want to bite her on the nose. My father's face stands between me and it.

'What's this boy doing here with you?'

'He's helping me just as you used to help your father.'

'He's doing me out of my share.'

'Your share goes to feed your brothers and sisters.'

'Then I'll feed off your nose.'

'Your pay's enough for you.'

'The tip of your nose will do me.'

'You haven't got a share.'

'Your nose is my share.'

'Hey! What are you doing?'

I pounced on her, twisting my fingers in her hair and holding on tight. I tried to raise her head so that I could bite her nose and was taken unawares by the taste of blood on my tongue. While we battled I noticed that her nose had been wounded, though I had not succeeded in tearing away any of it, not even the tiniest little bit. With loud wails she scratched at my face. I knocked her head against the wall. People collected, the place becoming as crowded as a bus. I was squeezed in between them. I told them she wouldn't pay her fare and must get off at the next stop. 'Where are your tickets? I know you—you're all trying to hide away in the crush so you won't pay, but I can tell only too well between the face that has paid and the back that hasn't.'

The crowd of people dragged us off to the police station. She told them I was mad and pointed to her bitten nose as evidence. She asked to be given police protection and that my brain should be examined. The sergeant drew up a report in which he included my name, address, age and occupation.

From that day on I knew they might be coming along any moment to take me off in a strait-jacket.

For a long time I walked doubled up, seeing that I had to be bent over like a bow inside my room—and also inside our company's buses. In doubling myself up like this I saved myself the effort of standing up straight. Also it was a way of hiding myself from people's eyes.

I used to try to hide from them and at the same time to prepare myself for encountering them. Every time I received my wages I would say: 'These are your last wages before they make off with you.' Every time I had a haircut I would say: 'This is the last haircut you'll have before they take you away.' Every time I had a bath I would say: 'This is the last time you'll bath before they put you in a strait-jacket.'

'Tickets.'

'Company employee.'

'Your card?'

The man takes out a card showing he's come out of a lunatic asylum. I ask him why he doesn't want to pay.

'Heavens!' he says, laughing. 'We're just the same!'

Ha ha ha! Ho ho ho!

I am Fathi Abdul Rasoul, bus conductor, poet, lover and lunatic. I wrote a song about crowds. My doctor doesn't believe I wrote it.

> In the crush bodies cling together, words cling,
> Conjoining and conjunctions both disappear,
> Relativity vanishes as do the relative pronouns.
> Crowds are a heavy burden, weighing down my heart, my back,
> Pressing against my flesh, creeping into the marrow of my
> bones.

I've seen people in a crush, have seen how dozens of them plunge forward frenziedly when there's a seat free. Some people are more skilled than others at edging their way through the masses of human flesh and it is they who win the seat or half-seat and sit down with a vague smile on their lips: like some minor local hero, an object of emulation and envy. But the nursing mothers and the pregnant, those who are too polite and those who hesitate and are too slow, go on standing, exuding bitterness, their hands tightly grasping the bar above them, like dangling human carcasses closely packed together. Ah! My joints ache. This is not in a song.

With me in this place are those who laugh and those who cry, those who are determined to stand for the rest of their lives on one foot, those who are determined to have one hand for ever raised. With me are the great of the world: Napoleon and Sayyid el-Badawi, and the owner of 'The Rocket Transport Companies Before the Invention of Rockets', which is the full name for his companies. We also have with us someone who has given himself the title of 'The Omnipotent'. They are all nice people except for Napoleon, who's the only one who frightens me. Whenever he gets hold of a stick he runs after me and tries to hit me, claiming that I'm a soldier who's mutinied and that he's punishing me with a marshal's baton; I run doubled up in front of him until the male nurses snatch the stick away from him.

As for the rest, they come from time to time to stand beside me to wait for the bus. Their patience, though, is soon exhausted and one after the other they steal away. Even the owner of The Rocket Transport Companies soon gives a snort and withdraws, while I stay on alone under the glare of the sun, waiting, waiting, waiting.

Ever since entering this place I've been telling myself: 'Tomorrow I'll leave.' Tomorrow and the day after and the day after that. Every year I say: 'This is the last anniversary celebration of Sidi Ahmed el-Nouti's I'll spend here. This is the last Prophet's Birthday. This is the last Lesser Bairam. This is the last Greater Bairam.'

Whenever I ask the doctor: 'When are you going to decide to let me out?' he replies: 'No, it's for you to decide—when you no longer see your father's face, when you stop biting women's noses, when you stand up straight again.' 'Is the city still overcrowded?' I ask him, and he laughs and says: 'You see, you're still not well.'

I see my doctor approaching with a new visitor. It is like this every day. I know him from his white coat and steel-rimmed glasses. I know what he's whispering to him, the same as he whispered to yesterday's visitor—and the day before yesterday and the day before that. He is assuring them that my joints are fine, that the illness is in the joints of my mind. Ha ha ha! He points at me saying: 'This bowed man is still waiting for the bus. For more than thirty years he has been standing and waiting, waiting for a place for himself in the crush of life.'

A Story from Prison

Yahya Hakki

The fact that it was a duty many times repeated did away with any
feelings the sergeant might have as he shoved those under arrest
into the cell. But with this particular man he was annoyed; with his
mouth screwed up and his grip cruelly tight, he enjoyed cursing
him and striking him on the back of the neck. It was not because
his eyes had alighted on legs that were sore and chapped, or that his
nose was assailed by a disgusting smell emanating from a dirty blue
galabia patched in numerous places with pieces of darker colours,
for he was accustomed to such things in the peasants who crossed
his path. Rather, it was because, ever since learning that the accused
was one of the band of gypsies the police had been after, he had
regarded him with an eye of repugnance. It was not the look one
man gave to another, but the scrutiny accorded by a superior species
to an inferior one. His hand had no sooner fallen on the other man's
shoulder than he was seized with a feeling of disgust that was close
to nausea. Gypsies! Were they human beings?

The gypsy entered the cell with a smile on his mouth brought
about by embarrassment, a smile that was cold and doltish and
became wider and more idiotic when his gaze alighted on a young
man sitting in a corner whom he saw was also smiling. Turning
his face away and squatting down in another corner, he proceeded
to think about himself so as to pass the time. His inactivity did not
last long. After a while he again glanced furtively at the young man,
gradually arousing in the latter a desire to enter into conversation.
The young man began by asking him his name, where he came from,
what he was charged with, and from there the conversation
branched out. The name of a famous criminal came up and he
mentioned that he knew him, that they were in fact distantly related.

'You're both from the same village?' asked the young man.

'Yes, he and I are from one and the same quarter.'

'I heard the policeman calling you a gypsy. How, then, was it you got mixed up with the gypsies if you used to be a peasant?'

The noise in the police-station courtyard grew louder as the sound of rifles being put into racks was heard, with here and there the crash of policemen's boots. A three-sentry patrol came along and sat down to talk alongside the prison cell. Their words reached the two men clearly, also their bursts of laughter. The gypsy drew closer to the young man till he was sitting beside him: he had not been friendly with a peasant for a long time. In the dreariness of prison and amidst the unusual hubbub, there was kindled in his heart a sympathy and affection for his companion. It may have been as a result of all these circumstances that he began to talk, neither evasively nor with anger. He was not so much recounting his story as reliving his past.

* * *

'I had rented from the omdah's brother fourteen *kirats* of land and I had a few head of sheep that I let loose in the fields in spring. When the Nile flood came I had no work, so the fellow with the land said to me: "Elaiwa, seeing as how you've nothing to do, why don't you go with my sheep up to Minya and take them along to a merchant I know there. You can take it from me, friend, I'll make it worth your while." I said to him: "The journey's too difficult for me." He replied: "You're experienced with sheep and I've chosen you—you're my man. The journey isn't as difficult as you think. Just keep along the Ibrahimiyya Canal, going northwards all the time, and you'll find yourself right on top of Minya." And the man went off, bought me a fine knife, gave me a donkey, and handed over sixty-five head of sheep. I went out of the village with them, with the floodwater lying a foot high on the fields, and continued driving the sheep ahead of me along the embankment of the Ibrahimiyya Canal.'

Sheep, though not timid animals, are not easily driven. They move slowly, and if not continually urged on come to a stop, and only a vigilant stick will bring together their scattered numbers. Sometimes Elaiwa would have to bring them together with his long cudgel to allow passage to approaching cars, while at others he would have to descend into the fields behind some stray ram. The whole day might well pass without his uttering more than a drawn-out, whistled shushing sound. With his long cudgel he would give sharp taps to the sheep's backs so as to bring them together into a single, easily managed flock, while their short, delicate feet stirred up a cloud of dust. Their cries of *ma . . . ma . . .* were continuous, some short and staccato, others almost a form of speech in which there was an unmistakable call for help. Some calls were harsh and husky, issuing from throats that had desiccated with the years, whereas others were like the twanging of the thin string of a musical instrument and emanated from small lambs, full of vivacity and exuberance, whose bellies were not yet distinguishable from their backs and whose mode of progression was by sideways leaps and playful buttings. A flock of sheep, too, bears within its folds the chain that binds life with death.

Elaiwa, fearing that a young lamb would lose its way, raised it up by its legs, at which it began bleating loudly and continuously. He walked along with it, cleaving himself a way amidst the sheep, every now and again lowering his hand so that it fell on a wave of wool set ablaze by the sun; the collected dust had liquefied with the animals' sweat, becoming hot and sticky above scalding bodies that bore their suffering with patience. When he reached the donkey, he opened a bag and placed the lamb inside. A skinny ewe, cleaving its way with an effort even greater than his own, had followed after him with a will that spoke of its determination not to be diverted by anything and which replied to each *ma* with an answer containing a tenderness that hid the loving concern of a mother.

Elaiwa's appearance gave no indication that he was capable of bearing the burden of looking after a flock of sheep, for he was a young man in his early youth. While one's eyes might not notice the signs of his Pharaonic ancestry—his tall stature and broad chest—they would not miss his obvious thinness and the lack of proportion between his large, splayed feet and spindly legs. Under his collar-bone was a hollow, possibly the result of hunger; from it rose two protruding bones at which the exposed hair of his chest ended. His face consisted of taut skin and muscle; whatever happened no spare flesh quivered there. When he moved his jaw, the surface of his temple was broken up into hollows and bumps. He was nevertheless ever on the go, his energy being renewed by some mysterious power that flowed in the Valley and was no less forceful than the Nile itself, a power that had not been crushed by building an idol like one of the Pyramids or been entombed by the passage of thousands of years.

Elaiwa would cover great distances with nothing remaining in his mind of the journey other than the names of the villages or the small white memorial domes set up to various holy men; some of these would lie high up on the canal embankment so that the village could bury its dead around them, while others would be down in the agricultural land flooded by the Nile so that the vegetation might benefit from their blessing. Elaiwa, like the peasant he was, and because he was making the journey for the first time, had little contact with the places he passed, nothing attracting his attention unless it affected him personally. Thus he was not at all impressed by the Ibrahimiyya Canal embankment, which looked ugly under the burning sun of Upper Egypt, screened by a thick cloud of dirt stretching out before him like a vast ribbon of piled-up, jagged-edged earth; continually rising and falling, its uneven surface was ever changing its mind as to whether to be narrow or broad. It was rendered even more ugly by the fact that it was much higher than the canal itself, so that nothing could be seen of the trees that had been planted at the water's edge except for short branches that blocked the view, branches which the person walking along the embankment could touch with his hand. What would Elaiwa say if someone were to tell him that much of the height of the embankment was not made up of earth, that deep within it there were also many skeletons of peasants, among them perhaps some of his own ancestors who had dug the canal across four provinces with their primitive picks, perhaps even with their nails? When a peasant died, the earth was piled on top of him, just as he was, with his basket, his pick and his one blue galabia. The canal had eaten up their bodies, wiping away their flesh and the lash marks on their skin.

'On the fourth day, just after the call to afternoon prayer, I reached Nazali Ganoub. I was intending to walk straight on and spend the night with the sheep in Senbu, but I don't know what it was that made me bring the sheep to a halt in front of this village. I'd be lying if I said I was tired—perhaps it was because I'd found a derelict mill on the embankment.'

The young man interrupted him in an almost sarcastic tone, like a man listening to a child:

'Or was it just your destiny that it happened like that?'

The young man was still smiling. His eyes never left Elaiwa whom he regarded as an entertaining spectacle, for ever since feeling that Elaiwa was treating him like a brother he had despised him. Whenever he interrupted the other's conversation with his mocking remarks—which was often—his body shook with pleasure.

'The Lord knows best. I didn't believe it when I found the mill had a big wall, so I got the sheep lined up and said to myself: "You're going to have a good night's sleep tonight, with no sheep escaping from you and you having to run around after them," so I settled myself down. When the time for evening prayer had come, I went close by the sheep, and taking off my galabia and putting my head on my arm, I went off to sleep. My eye hadn't yet met up with sleep before I found a group of people making their way towards me from the direction of the village. In their midst were a couple of donkeys, also some goats going in front of them. When they got up to me I found they were a band of gypsies. I said to myself: "What rotten bad luck, but maybe, old chap, they'll go straight on." I got up and hid myself so as to see what would happen. They came right alongside me and stopped. After a while I found them spreading out their bedding around me.'

Two men went to the donkeys and unloaded thin screens, which they leant up against each other—and there, in front of Elaiwa, were two small tents. They knocked some pegs into the ground to which they tied their goats. A woman took out a cooking-pot and sat down rubbing it clean with earth, then went to the canal. One of them brought out three pieces of stick tied up in a bundle. He unfolded them, fixing their feet in the ground, and brought along a kettle, which he hung in the middle, lighting a fire beneath it and leaning his head forward and blowing at it. After a while there was the smell of tea and the gypsies became aware of their neighbour.

'One of them said to me: "Please have a drink of tea with us," so I got up, went over and sat down.'

'Had it been a long time since you drank tea?' the young man asked him.

'You know that peasants are stupid and won't say "No" to any invitation. But to tell you the truth, I was frightened, what with all

those stories in our village about gypsies being thieves and kidnappers and playing tricks you'd never even think of. I said to
myself: "My boy, take a good look at those people." They had with
them a girl who went backwards and forwards in front of me. I
only noticed her when I saw the men frowning at her. Not one of
them would speak to her in a decent, friendly way, all the time shouting and snapping at her. Sometimes she'd answer back, sometimes
walk off in silence. I don't know what she'd done to them that they
should swear at her behind her back, saying such things as: "You
crazy thing, you'll see, we'll show you." After that, every time she
passed in front of me I'd take a look at her.'

He found she had a dark brown face, almost completely round,
and a thin nose; she was tattooed on her forehead with a green spot
and on her chin with a foliate design. She was short and straight-
backed, and the way she was constantly moving her head showed a
very nervous disposition. She would hide her anger by visibly
pressing down on her lips, which made them thinner and wider.
When she came to pass round the glasses a smell that was alien to
his nose was wafted from her to him, a mixture of sweat and dirt
and a perfume containing carnation and wormwood. Before he
knew it Elaiwa was engaged in conversation with them.

'We went on talking and they went on asking me about the sheep:
Where was I taking them? How many had I got? I was frightened
they were taking my mind off things because of some plot they had.
I said to myself: "Get up and guard your sheep." I went back to my
place but wasn't able to sleep. No sooner had my eyes closed in
sleep well after midnight than I was woken by the barking of the
dog and found that my sheep were all scattered about in front of
three policemen whose horses' eyes gleamed like sparks in the darkness. I can still recall them now. I went crazy, running about and
falling over. Every time I turned in the direction of the gypsies I
found the policemen breaking up the tents, with the fire out and
turned to smoke. I heard them being cursed: "Thieves—kidnappers
—sons of bitches." Their arms were waving above their heads as
they screamed: "Have mercy, Sergeant." It was no good, though—
they rounded them up on a chain, and I went on gathering up the
sheep until, thanks be to the Lord, I got them all together. I went
back to my place and was about to take off my galabia and go to
sleep when I looked out and found the gypsy girl rolled up in a

heap right up against the wall. To tell you the truth, I trembled from the shock of it. What a business! What calamity had befallen me?

'"Girl, you here? What's brought you? What are you doing?"'

'She motioned to me to keep quiet until the policemen had all gone. She then threw herself at my feet, saying:

'"I'm at your mercy—those men wanted to kill me. They thought I gave them away. In the Kousiyya robbery they put us all in prison, and directly they came out they stole again. I beseech you to take me with you. I'll go wherever you go, just so long as I get away from those people."'

The gypsy girl stretched out her arms and clasped him round the neck. Neither trembling nor breathing quickly, the only thing that had changed in her was that the tightness of her lips had disappeared and they now looked swollen and revealed two large teeth. Her eyes drooped. Was it that he was tired, or was it because it was Elaiwa's first experience? Perhaps, too, it was because he had never before smelt at close quarters the scent of carnation and wormwood. Whatever the reason, Elaiwa felt his strength melt away between her hands and his arms drop limply to his side. There came back to his mind the image of this woman passing in front of him as he sat drinking tea with her companions and he remembered the way she had of tossing her head. He did not then realize—though he does now—that these tossings of the head had an extraordinary attraction for him, a powerful fascination. His silence lasted a long time, and he analysed it as being an effect of his upbringing which had taught him since he was young to stand in awe and fear of gypsies. But he did not repel the woman's arms; in fact after a while he had the sensation that the numbness in his nerves had been replaced by a throbbing in his forehead, a dryness in his throat and a trembling in his heart. All these things combined to fill his veins with blood that boiled and thundered in his ears. He took her hands in his and was further inflamed by having her draw gradually closer to him, impelled towards him by a feeling that was a mixture of joy and defiance. Maybe her passion was not for the man but resulted from savouring the pleasure of her freedom on this her first night. No sooner had the man returned her embrace than there burst forth from its hiding-place a strong desire that had long been suppressed, and in its unloosening a tornado was set free. It was none the less careful not to expend itself too quickly, curbing its impetuosity and veiling its vehemence with a screen of deliberation and poise. Her whole concern was to give the man what he had not previously had, and to take from him the maximum possible. As his mouth lay on hers there shone in her eyes—despite the darkness—the image of conquest. Were instinct to have had a body and were it to have looked down upon them, it would have nodded its head in pride and satisfaction, and it would have excused itself for this by saying that while it was not happy about the bashful and timid manner in which most people indulge their instinct, there were, here and there, at different times, a few individuals who realized its full potential, persons who gave up their very souls to it and allowed themselves to be wholly possessed by it. The kiss did not last long, for the woman came to her senses and became aware of where she was; she therefore rose to her feet and, drawing the man by the hand, entered through a gap in the wall of the mill, where the darkness wrapped them round. This night it was for the dog, together with the sheep, to guard their master.

'To cut a long story short, she spent the night with me. I said to her: "My good girl, I am a God-fearing man and I want to have the blessing of the law." She said: "I have given myself to you." I said to her: "I accept, and if anyone hears about this I'll say that many peasants marry in country towns purely by mutual consent."'

'But on the embankment they don't,' said his friend, 'and not with gypsies.'

'At the time I didn't know what I was about.'

He did not know how he had gone to sleep. When day came he found himself not the master of a flock but the slave of a fate whose staff made no distinction in the way it drove both human beings and sheep. Despite this, he felt that this woman had bestowed upon him a pleasure that was new to him: like a tired man he had been led to her, finding after his exertions a comfortable bed. Elaiwa let himself relax and rely upon her, not caring, in this honeyed state of lethargy, what fetters she bound him with so long as the stream of vitality that had awakened in him—and which thereafter he was unable to curb—found no other outlet but her in which to swell and pour forth. Elaiwa forgot the days of his past and confined his attention to the moment he was in and in the morning he would walk off, still in a state of bewilderment, behind his flock.

'Again we went off at dawn, with me in a daze. We made Daryout

—no, no, I forgot, after we'd been walking a while I looked round for the dog and didn't find it. I went back to look for it and found it near a tree in the throes of death.'

The dog was lying with its hindquarters on the ground, its head raised on quivering forepaws, its body shaken with convulsions. The dog stared at its master, and in its eyes there shone a momentary gleam of hope, which was quickly extinguished by a deep and silent sadness. He had never before seen eyes weeping like the glassy, staring ones of the dog, talking to him and saying: 'Will this be the last time you see me?' It opened its mouth, but death placed his hand over it and the dog was unable to bark. Instead of a yelp there flowed from it streams of viscid slaver that told of the unknown pain that boiled in the animal's stomach. Elaiwa did not understand the reason for what had happened. Perhaps someone had beaten it, for many was the peasant who cruelly beat stray dogs, or perhaps some young boy had thrown a stone at it—this act of lust which the first criminal tendency in a child's head puts into practice. He stretched out his hand to run it across the dog's back and found it undamaged. He felt the gypsy girl by his side.

'She had come to sit beside me and watch. I looked at her and she said to me: "My people have poisoned it—they wanted to steal your sheep while you were asleep. They weren't given the time, the Devil take them. Don't be angry, tomorrow you'll find another one. And just so you'll feel better I've brought you two of their goats—they are those two in the middle." I said to her: "Are they yours, the two goats?" She said to me: "No, they're theirs."'

The young man again interrupted him:

'Got yourself a bit of loot for nothing.'

'By Allah, I wasn't happy about taking them but what could I do . . . ?'

Just as his dog, lying between the hands of death, had been unable to bark, so he, between the hands of the woman who had stolen his mind, was unable to open his mouth. Nothing was more expressive of the difference between their two natures than the slight smile which played on the gypsy girl's mouth and was matched by a perceptible frown on the peasant's brow.

The dog's trembling grew less, little by little, until its movements ceased altogether and the flies dared to settle on its mouth and eyes. As Elaiwa rose to return to his flock, there contended within him grief for the dog he was leaving behind and a feeling of dread at the two goats that walked in front of him and which embodied the first crime he had ever committed; he who had lived all his years in awe of the police-station, who shook before the omdah and would greet policemen with respect.

'From the first day I found that the gypsy girl was clever. She would save the milk she used to draw off, and sell it. In the past I hadn't known what to do with it. Also she weaned several lambs for me, having fixed a bag on each of the ewes. I had forgotten about the two goats. I said to myself: "Tomorrow, my lad, you'll return to your village and you'll raise your own sheep, and if you've got yourself a girl as clever as this one why not accept other people's sheep and keep them with you and graze them. Tomorrow, my lad, you'll get yourself a better living—your Lord is generous."

'After several days I got to Mallawi and found at the entrance to the town some bare land. I left the sheep there and went up to the embankment opposite a café and sat down. The girl disappeared below with the sheep. Right from the beginning the night was a lousy one. I don't know what came over the girl during it—she had turned completely against me by the morning.'

The gypsy girl had gone down to walk slowly among the ewes: there was nothing to keep her with the flock, likewise nothing to prompt her to return to Elaiwa.

She had begun to be bored with her new regulated life that proceeded along a known course and she yearned again for her old nomadic existence. Her whole pleasure lay in being hounded from one village to another, her link with each place not exceeding a single night. The initial passion had waned and there was now nothing more to Elaiwa than a peaceful man whose goodness she could be sure of, and she felt nostalgia for a life that was half love and half hate. The gypsies are egoists and do not accept strangers in their midst. She had continued to submit to one of their men, not from love but through necessity, and she used to find her pleasure in the continual struggle between her passionate nature and her bitter dislike of him. What greater pleasure was there than refusing to submit until after a flood of desire had risen up to her mouth almost drowning her and making her forget her dislike, great though it might be? Whenever fulfilment coincides with breaking point the spirit enjoys the most sublime extremes of ecstasy. For the present she submitted, be the flood at her feet or at her knees; she did not know the pleasure of satiety because she had been deprived of the pleasure of being hungry. While not hating Elaiwa, she would have liked him to have been a gypsy.

The light of a lamp that lit up the embankment where Elaiwa was sitting cut through the gypsy girl's thoughts. A café came into view, in the centre of which and under a lamp was a wooden dais where a man sat with a two-stringed fiddle, singing. She forgot her thoughts and came up to listen to the story of how 'Imprisoned were Marei, Yahya and Younis, at the palace of Zanati in Tunis', and 'The return of Prince Abu Zeid to the ruins'. The man let out a succession of shouts at which the murmurings of those seated abated and all gave ear to the story and the poetry. As the night drew on the breathing of the lamp grew more constricted, choked by a thick circle of mosquitoes that, despite the rising smoke, had congealed like dirt around it. The universe was wrapped round in total silence; the sky in its darkness was like the wings of a bat that has alighted on the earth. From time to time it gave a slight shudder, the result of the vibration of those few stars that flicker and then grow still. Neither the lamp with its hissing, nor the singer with his fiddle, was able to disperse any of the sadness that oppressed the universe. Was night the corpse of day and this sadness the hymn of death? Or was the world in mourning because it sensed it was perishing little by little? Or perhaps it was as a result of the thousands of Oriental souls created by God sad and sore of heart that wander about this vast expanse? This very same sky, when covering the north, is perhaps the epitome of joy, fulfilment and ecstasy, and the flickering of its stars is a dance.

This atmosphere weighed heavily upon the fiddle, which gave out a monotonously plaintive sound. The whole world stood on one side, the fiddle on the other, and a dialogue took place between them, each one giving up its secrets to the other. So affected by the story were the listeners that the singer disappeared from their view and Abu Zeid took shape before them, sitting on the dais letting out his warlike cries at them. Times became so mixed up in their minds, that they did not know whether it was he who had been brought back to life to recount to them the stories of his battles, or they who had been transported by some magic hand to his distant age. The poet chose an ode he knew from experience would make an impres-

sion on his audience, and he ended his evening with it. The last
verses he sang were:

> O woe, my heart, at what happened
>   When with six fetters separation shackled me.
> Outwitted by the worries that to me came,
>   When will those old days return?
> Destiny's voice answered me saying:
>   Time that has passed will ne'er again return.
> Weep, O eye, for the time that has passed,
>   Your recompense is from Allah the One, the Adored.

Did the anonymous poet know, as he described the sufferings of
his heroes, that his poetry would be heard by this gypsy girl on the
embankment and that she would receive it like a knife-thrust? Maybe he knew this and more than this, or otherwise how was it that he
spoke out what was in her innermost being as though he already
knew her, had been associated with her, and had heard her griev-
ance many times? Her eyes watered with copious tears, then her
stubbornness and unruliness awoke and she suppressed her worries.
She got up to go to sleep, having resolved to carry out the idea that
had been occupying her mind those last few days.

'I woke from sleep and found her walking along the embankment, her galabia hitched up under her arm. She was walking slowly
but I realized immediately that she was escaping from me. I went
running after her, caught up with her, and seized her by the arm:

'"Where are you going?"

'"Walking. . . ."

'"Where to?"

'"To the west of the mountain, maybe I'll be able to join my
people there."

'"By yourself?"

'"Yes, let me go my way and you yours."

'"My dear girl, I've told you the sheep aren't mine, their owner
is in Minya which is now no more than a stone's throw from us,
after which I'm returning immediately with you to the village."

'"Your village and all that's in it can go to hell," she told me then
and there.'

The young man stared at Elaiwa as though expecting the angry
outburst of a peasant who accepts everything but the insulting of

his kinsfolk. However, Elaiwa had by that time been almost completely separated from his family and kinsfolk; the insult did not arouse his sensitivity and he swallowed it.

'I said to her,' Elaiwa went on: "Let's not go to the village. All right, we'll go anywhere you want."

'"Come with me."

'"And the sheep?"

'"Bring them with you."

'"They're not mine."

'As though annoyed at what I'd said she sharply averted her face. She walked off again and was nearly out of sight. While all this was happening the Devil was trying to turn my head.'

Elaiwa had stopped there with every vein in him pulsating and alert. Her impetuosity had intoxicated him, had made him lose his head. He cast a glance at the woman, then a glance at the flock of sheep, while the Devil stood in front of him, smiling and holding the balance. The scale came down on the side of the woman.

'"Slow up," I shouted at her. "Slow up, I'm coming."

'I ran to the sheep and drove them from the embankment to another road leading to the west of the mountain, and we walked off without giving the world a thought. I really didn't know where it was all going to end.

'That night I saw her do something extraordinary. We were passing by a farm and found a hen pecking about in the road. The girl took out from her pocket a long piece of thread with a grain of maize tied on the end. She threw it in front of the hen, which picked it up. It stuck in its throat and the hen began scraping its beak on the ground. It wanted to cry out but couldn't. The girl pulled it towards her very gradually and put it under her arm. Directly we'd put a distance between ourselves and the village she killed it. We got to the mountain. . . .'

'Wait a bit—who ate the chicken?'

'We ate it together.'

'Why was it the girl didn't pull this trick before?'

'How should I know? This food was like poison to me and I asked Allah for His protection.'

'You're right there—someone who steals sixty-five head of sheep is hardly going to have any qualms about a chicken.'

Elaiwa was silent and sighed loud and long. The moon had disappeared and the glow from a lamp hanging some way off reached the solitary prison cell in the middle of the station courtyard. The loud thumping of horses' hooves on the asphalt rang out and a donkey brayed alongside them. Then the place quietened down again and Elaiwa, with broken heart, returned to his story. His affection for his companion had waned, preoccupied as he was with himself as he recounted his adventures in brief: he was not reliving his past so much as remembering with an effort some of what had happened to him.

'On the mountain we met her band. She was alone with their leader for a while. God knows what they were saying about me. I saw her pointing to the sheep and the man looking at them as though he were counting them. I went off with the sheep. Two or three days later I found that the sheep were one head missing. I must say my blood really boiled. I got hold of the girl and said to her: "If someone doesn't want to lose his life he'd better not go near the sheep."

'"We're now gypsies together," she said. "All our belongings are together." I said to her: "Gypsies or not, I don't hold with such talk." She screwed her mouth up at me and continued not to talk to me. After a couple of days I went to her and said: "My good girl, I've sold my people and my honour for you." Though she made it up with me, she was really having me on. Every other moment she would say to me: "Don't be afraid for your sheep, gypsies don't steal from one another." Even so, every time we came near a market I'd find one or two head of sheep missing. She had lied to me. . . .'

'She hadn't lied to you, it was you who'd considered yourself a gypsy while they didn't consider you one. That's why they were stealing from you. You were booty for them, fair game.'

'The sheep ended up at ten, then five. I said to myself: "What's it all about, lad? Will you be left with nothing at all?" One night I fooled them and got up before dawn and drove away those that were left and went to the market, where I sold them and took myself off.'

'You fooled them? After all, weren't the sheep yours?'

Elaiwa did not reply but continued with his story:

'About a week ago they bundled me off and they stole—we stole together—a sack of cotton from a field. Yesterday night we were arrested.'

It was inevitable that Elaiwa should taste some of the insults and harassment that gypsies experience. The night when the horsemen had attacked, the lashes had fallen and the handcuffs been fastened, had come and gone. However, spending time in the company of gypsies had made him able to accept abuse, handcuffs and the lash with equanimity. A year ago he had been a witness to what had befallen the gypsies and his terror, as a spectator, had been greater than it was today as, after a beating, he walked in chains to the police-station. In the year that had passed it was not so much his life that had been consumed as his morals and habits that had been demolished. He had been a peasant whose concern was with the Nile, the omdah, the police-station and the boundaries of the land which he would measure by span of hand and length of finger. As for now, he was a gypsy concerned only with the day he was in: the whole world was before him and it had no boundaries. If he was able to get something from it, then he should grab it. He was happy.

'And the police brought her with you?' the young man asked him.

'The girl? No, she got away again.'

'Let's hope this time round she doesn't find someone else to bring down.'

'No, where will she find anyone? Directly I'm out I'll go off and start looking for her.'

This time the young man did not make fun of him. Yawning and stretching, he lay down on the ground. Before going to sleep he recited in a low voice, without singing it, this mawwal:

Can you leave your beloved
    Even if, O the pity, she has done you wrong
Or filled your glass with bitterness,
    Stirred it round and given it you to drink?
No, not even if she's raised a stick against you
    And, woe betide you, has driven you before her.
Night, O night, thus is my fate. . . .

The Child and the King

Gamil Atia Ibrahim

His childhood was spent in Old Cairo where he lived near the Mosque of Amr ibn al-Aas. After the sunset prayer he would go to the mosque to accompany his father back home, while during the day he would play in the square. In the month of Ramadan he would dream of seeing the King when he came to pray there on the last Friday of the month.

To him the King was capable of everything, was strong as a train, as high as the stars; he could handle fire without fear, could fly in the air, could drink up all the water in the Nile. Every year the child would be driven out of the square in the early morning when the sweepers' carts arrived; he would return home in tears and stand on the balcony, among the very young and the very old, while the grown-ups successfully broke through the barrier of policemen to take their stand in the front rows right near the King. He would have a feeling of anger and hatred for those grown-ups, and would spend the whole of that day riding round the house on a small piece of stick, in imitation of those men astride their horses during the long hours of the ceremony.

The memory of that ceremony—with its crowds, colours and music—would remain in his mind for several months; he would talk of it joyfully, and whenever he looked towards the square he would see, in his mind's eye, the coloured flags and hear the soldiers marching.

On the morning of the 27th July, when the news of the King having been ousted and being forced to leave the country was spread abroad, he went to the square. He found everything quiet and calm; in a state of depression, he approached the walls of the mosque and found them bare of all decoration, as yellow and sombre as the walls of the kitchen. He learnt from the boys in the street that the King had travelled away on a ship, a big ship that had many rooms, with a cinema and a football pitch, and that he had taken his wife and children with him. For the first time he came to know that the King was married and had small children who would make pee-pee all over him. He was a bit annoyed because he had always thought that the King was not married.

When his father came home in the evening, he began questioning him about the King. The man was tired and didn't have a long talk with him as he usually did. The young child understood nothing of what he said, though he did intuitively grasp the fact that a revolution was like a train or a plane and swept away everything standing in its path.

The young child began to make up to his father, but in the end preferred to go off in silence to a corner of the room.

'The King's gone to Italy,' he heard him saying to his mother.

The child asked about Italy.

'It's far away,' said the man.

The child was astonished at this revolution which could oust the King, that strong, fat man with the thick moustaches he saw in pictures. Before his father had finished putting on his clothes, he asked him what 'revolution' meant.

The man, at the end of his patience, replied:

'Revolution means government.'

The child did not know what government meant either.

Before the man had put his shoes on, the child asked him about the ceremony that used to take place on the last Friday in Ramadan, at which the man began telling him in a tone both tender and grave that prayers were said to God alone and that Muslims performed their prayers whether the King attended or not.

The child did not believe his father and jumped up shouting:

'Long live the King! Long live the King!'

The man began hitting his young son with his shoe, telling him to shut up and repeating the one word *revolution*.

The child understood that something important had taken place. In fear he went off to his mother; in tears, he threw himself upon her, grasping her round the knees.

'They say,' said the man, 'that the King was a thief and that the people are glad he's gone.'

The child remembered the celebration—the cheering, the flags and the music—and he shivered in his mother's embrace and shouted: 'Long live the King!' Then he buried his face in her bosom as he broke into sobs. His mother kissed him tenderly, while the man stayed where he was in a state of fright.

The mother, determined to put an end to this fear, got up and switched on the wireless. For the first time she turned up the volume. Singing voices poured forth from the wireless, blaring out into the room and rocking it. The child understood nothing of these songs that rejoiced in the revolution. Directly the music came to an end, he jumped up shouting:

'Long live the King!'

The mother went up to the frightened man and tried to put his mind at rest.

'He's only young,' she said, 'and understands nothing about politics.'

'There are now Pashas and nobles in the prisons,' said the man, 'but we're poor.'

'We're from the people,' said the woman stolidly.

The child understood nothing of what his mother had said. However, he felt that the revolution was like a train, that it crushed everything under its wheels.

*   *   *

Later on the child went to school and learnt a lot about the King and the revolution. He forgot about those celebrations. After finishing at the university, he went into politics. He would make fun of his elderly father who sat in the café and recounted to his friends how he had supported the revolution from the beginning, and how he had led a demonstration in its support on the very day the King was thrown out . . . for the son knew that his father was a liar.